EASTER PROMISES

AN HISTORICAL ANTHOLOGY

CLARE GRIFFIN   SARAH FIDDELAERS

NANCY CUNNINGHAM   AVA JANUARY

Easter Promises: An Historical Anthology

First published 2020

Easter Dawn © 2020 Sarah Fiddelaers

An Easter Lily on the Somme © 2020 Nancy Cunningham

Le Malin Renard © 2020 Ava January

Eos © 2020 Clare Griffin

Published by

Girl On A Soapbox Press

BAYSWATER VIC 3153

AUSTRALIA

Cover image from Adobe Photos

Designed by Lana Pecherczyk

Paperback ISBN: 978-0-9945333-3-3

Digital ISBN 978-0-9945333-2-6

❀ Created with Vellum

‽

To all the readers who have gone before us, especially
Judy Cooney,
Jessie Cunningham,
and SMG.

‽

EASTER DAWN

~

By Sarah Fiddelaers

CHAPTER 1

Wyndam House, Widuwe Island, Victoria, Australia
Shrove Tuesday, 1912

The motor pulled away from the village station and Eric settled back into the cushions. He fixed his gaze out the window as the car drove away from the village, through the clutter of fisherman's houses on the flats by the shore. The late summer sun was beginning to set. Anxious wives were keeping watch at their front gates, children about their skirts. The women's eyes probed the ocean that foamed by the heads, watching for the boats to come safely through the rough waters.

But Eric's gaze was focused east, on the tower across the bay that peeped over the top of the Norfolk pines rimming the island of Widuwe.

Wyndam House glowed a soft pink as the setting sun caressed the sandstone facade and Eric sighed, his shoulders settling. The granite in his chest felt lighter. Widuwe had always felt more like home to him than anywhere else. The first glimpse as the motor approached the causeway that ran from the mainland to the little island in the bay was his favourite part of the journey. From habit his eyes sought the window on the third floor where he knew she would be watching for him. Where she had watched for him since they were children.

But they weren't children anymore. He was nearly finished his medical studies and she—but here Eric's thoughts stalled and he looked away from the window. His chest grew heavy again. He didn't have the right to indulge in such dreams about Minnie Wyndam. The anger that had curdled his insides for the past month flared and his hand clenched into a fist and knocked against his thigh. He wouldn't have agreed to come tonight had he been able to think of any way to refuse. But he owed it to Minnie to say goodbye, little though she would understand.

How differently he had thought these last few weeks of his university career would play out. But instead of signalling the beginning of his independence and the freedom to finally court Minnie in earnest, his final exams in a few weeks' time would be the beginning of the end of everything he knew. Eric's jaw tightened as he thought of what this evening would be if it weren't for his changed circumstances. His gaze drifted back to Minnie's window. She was standing there watching, he could see her outline. As the car swept off the causeway and under the whispering sheoaks to climb the drive, she raised a hand and waved at him.

The Wyndam family and several of the dinner guests were gathered in the drawing room when Eric was announced.

'Tell me,' said Eleanor McCrae, standing next to Minnie, 'when are you coming to town? We've ordered invitations for my ball from the printers, and Mama is planning a breakfast and a picnic for later in the season.'

Minnie tore her gaze away from where Eric was chatting to her parents and summoned a smile, taking a breath to still the furious beat of wings in her chest.

'After Easter. We have a house party Easter Weekend.' Minnie's eyes flickered towards Eric again, but she couldn't catch his eye. 'And then we'll come to town and begin preparations for the season. Mama has engaged Lucy Secor to make my gowns, but I haven't been to see her yet.'

'Lucky you,' said Eleanor, eying Minnie's gown while fidgeting with the lace at her bodice. 'I simply *begged* to have Lucy make my gowns, but mama wouldn't hear of it. So I have to endure this frightful old woman who jabs me with pins and yells at me in French. Is this one of hers?'

'Yes,' Minnie dragged her eyes away from where Eric was now laughing at something her brother Jack was saying. She smoothed her gloved hand down the skirt of her gown, a white silk overlaid with pale pink chiffon. She wore a pink pleated satin waistband with the chiffon draped over the bodice, parting to reveal delicate silver embroidery on the white silk underneath.

'Mama wanted to be sure she was everything she'd been reported to be, so we had this made. It's a Lucille pattern.'

'You'll be the toast of the season,' said Eleanor enviously, 'and everyone will think I'm someone's poor relation.'

Minnie smiled, knowing that since Eleanor was a member of Melbourne's oldest and most well-respected family, her success for her first season was assured.

'Have you thought how mortifying it would be to be a failure in your first season?' Minnie asked Eleanor, and then laughed at her friend's look of confusion. 'Of course you haven't, you already know everyone. I don't want to be the toast of the season, as you put it, but I don't want people I've met three times to look through me, either. Do you know, when we came to town for the Australia Day ball at the Menzies Hotel, I had no fewer than three odious people, when introduced to me, nod politely and give me the most *crushing* snubs. Because they didn't recognise my surname.'

'Oh Minnie,' said Eleanor, laughing, 'you don't need to worry about those people. The merest provincials. Anyone who knows anything knows your parents, even if they live mostly out of the world now a days. People who snub you because they don't recognise your surname are probably encroaching sorts of people. Trying to protect their stupid dignity from others doing exactly what they themselves are doing. Foisting themselves onto a society that doesn't want them. Now tell me, when is your ball to be? Did Lady Wyndam absolutely forbid the masquerade?'

'Yes of course she did,' said Jack Wyndam, joining them and bringing Eric with him, 'it's too racy apparently.'

'Oh that's a shame,' said Eleanor.

Minnie made a non-committal noise. Her eyes were on Eric and the hummingbird in her chest was trilling happily.

'Hello Minnie,' he said, meeting her eyes briefly, smiling at her with the warmth she had come to crave. But behind the smile, he looked tired, and the eyes that were usually bright with laughter were shadowed. His face had a closed expression she had never seen him wear before. She found herself suddenly shy of him. The hummingbird in her chest stilled its wings.

The great ballroom of Wyndam House was situated on the ground floor at the back of the house. After dinner the guests were ushered into a magnificent space adorned with flowers and treated, on three sides, to views of the last of the summer light disappearing over the mainland and ocean. The French doors that led out to the terrace and the south lawn were thrown open, letting a gentle onshore breeze mix with the heady scents of the flowers and refresh the otherwise close atmosphere of the ballroom.

In the dwindling evening light, many lanterns could be seen bobbing on the bay as the rest of the guests, all arrived on the special train from Melbourne, were ferried across from the village to the Widuwe pier. It was one of the most popular parts of the evening, the twilight boat ride across to the island sitting fairy-like and serene in the gathering dusk.

As the band struck up 'Valse Septembre' Minnie busied herself making introductions amongst the debutantes and the men who had made up the dinner guests. She herself could not dance until all the young girls had found a partner, and she did not intend to sit out more dances than she could help.

She kept half an eye on Eric as she moved about the ballroom, her heart uncomfortable in her chest. Though never backwards in any attention, he had been reserved throughout dinner, and the shadows had not left his eyes. She had not been the only one to notice.

'What's gotten into Eric?' Eleanor asked her when Minnie had matched as many dance couples as she could.

Minnie sipped her iced lemonade and watched Eric lead one of the debutantes to the dance floor, his face expressionless. 'I don't know. Perhaps it's the stress of his final exams. They're only a matter of weeks away.'

'I've never seen him so glum, and I saved a dance for him. He'd better not frown at me through the whole set,' said Eleanor with a grimace.

'He's tired of you all,' said a voice from behind them. Minnie felt her heart sink in her chest. She turned to face Nellie Radcliffe, the flat haired, mean tongued daughter of the dean of Melbourne University.

'Hello Nellie,' she said, trying to remember she was in part hostess this evening.

'What are you doing here, Nellie?' asked Eleanor, not bothering to hide her dislike. 'I would have thought that your socialist sympathies would be offended by the very thought of enjoying yourself at a ball.'

'I didn't come to enjoy myself. I came to support Eric.'

Minnie and Eleanor looked at each other.

'Support him in what way?' Minnie asked.

'Support him through the ordeal of an evening spent in the colourless company of pretty ninnies like the two of you,' said Nellie, pursing her lips in what Minnie supposed was her attempt at a smile. Eleanor shook her head.

'I'm needed for the first dance,' she said, turning her back on Nellie and rolling her eyes at Minnie. Minnie tried to frown her into staying, but Eleanor winked at her and sashayed across the ballroom. More than one man followed her with his eyes as she moved to claim her dance partner.

'All of this,' said Nellie, sweeping a disdainful arm that encompassed the house and everyone in it, 'is not real. None of it actually matters.'

'You don't think so?' asked Minnie, mentally abusing Eleanor for abandoning her to Nellie's wrath.

'You and your little golden-haired friend twittering together like birds about the fine clothes you'll wear to the grand parties you will go to, what does any of it matter?'

'We cannot all be blessed with your indifference to appearances, dear Nellie,' said Minnie sweetly. Nellie's eyes narrowed and she leaned in closer to Minnie.

'To a man like Eric, who's been out in the world, learning skills to help people, guide them through illness, save them from death, improve their lot, do you think that matters? What is there to keep him in a shallow world like this?'

Minnie felt as though she'd been slapped. The humming-bird in her chest dug its claws into her flesh.

'This world is becoming too small for Eric. It's time for him to quit it. He longs for a purpose, and he will not find it in your precious gilded halls.'

ELEANOR, Minnie knew, would laugh at her if she knew how deeply Nellie's words affected her. But for Minnie, the ball lost all its pleasure from the moment she parted from Nellie. She joined the first dance and smiled and laughed and danced like everyone else, but her mind was busy with worry and the doubts she had thought banished returned with renewed strength.

Supper was held out on the terrace overlooking the south lawn. The garden had been lit with flickering lamps and the ocean, though no longer visible, kept them company with its murmurs. As the guests enjoyed the wild roast duck, oysters and Cook's famous French crepes, Minnie slipped away from the crowd and took a turn about the lamp-lit garden, giving vent to her seething nerves.

Were it not for the change in Eric, she would have dismissed Nellie's comments as foolishness. But he was altered, even Eleanor had said as much. Something had gone amiss, and it seemed that Nellie saw herself as the answer.

A heat, not entirely due to the warmth of the night, crept into Minnie's cheeks as she remembered the eagerness with which she had appraised her reflection earlier in the evening, hoping that her dress and hair and appearance would all be to Eric's liking. Her heart had been full of their last meeting, and the closeness that had grown between them. Not the camaraderie of time spent growing up together, but the understanding of two who were now adults together, he a gentleman and she a lady. A lump formed in her throat. It seemed that the understanding had all been a thing of her imagination.

She reached the end of the walk and came to a clearing that overlooked the southern slope of the island and out over the ocean towards the heads of Port Phillip Bay. The lights of the village lighthouse and those further along the coast could be seen sweeping across the night.

She stood looking into the darkness, listening to the hush hush of the ocean and gentle thud of sailboats against the wood of the pier. She could not rid herself of Nellie's question. What was there to keep a man like Eric in this world of gaiety?

A step sounded behind her and she turned quickly to see

a man striding up the path, his gaze on his feet. It was Eric. She knew him before she saw him properly.

'Another escapee,' she said, trying to keep her tone light around the lump in her throat.

He paused. She could tell she'd surprised him.

'Minnie—!' he said, and there was something like relief in his tone.

'I had to remove myself from the crepes,' she said, 'before I was outed as a glutton.'

'I think Jack's eaten most of them,' he said coming to stand beside her.

Minnie wanted to reach out and put her hand on his arm. The need to touch him, to anchor him to this place, to *her*, was overwhelming. The lump in her throat pushed against her windpipe. She was not used to hiding her thoughts from Eric.

'I had an interesting conversation with Miss Radcliffe,' she said, looking up at Eric in the dark. She could see his profile outlined against the glow that came from the house. 'She seemed to intimate that you are going away from us all. I didn't quite understand her meaning.'

Eric sighed and looked down, then turned to Minnie.

'I'm not going away, precisely, but I've turned down my uncle's offer for a place in his Collins Street practice. I'm going into the Women's Hospital instead.'

Minnie frowned into the dark.

'The charity hospital?' she asked, trying to envisage such a place.

'Yes, the charity hospital,' said Eric. His voice hardened and Minnie bit her lip. The hospital and the messy, complicated problems of the humanity that came through the doors was a far cry from the refined world of Eric's uncle's genteel practice.

'That's quite a decision.'

'It was supposed to be a private one,' said Eric.

'Your father—?'

'I haven't told him.'

'Will he cut you off?'

'There's no question about it. He'd be glad of the excuse. I'll be on my own. Nellie's father has arranged for me to train under Dr Tracy, lecturer in obstetric medicine. He spends some of his time doing house calls in the poorer areas, which I plan to do with him. I want to make a difference, Min. To do something truly useful. The slums in Melbourne, you have no idea how desperate some people's lives are. If I can make even a particle of difference, then I have to do it.'

'Could you not do the same thing working for your uncle?'

'No.'

The anger in Eric's voice surprised her. Minnie looked at him inquiringly, but he wouldn't meet her eyes. They were silent for a long time, standing there with only the sounds of the ocean between them.

'You know how it works, Minnie,' said Eric eventually. 'I'll be something of an outcast, but it doesn't worry me. This is more important than having my name on all the invitation lists.'

'You'll miss the season,' said Minnie, and knew immediately that it had come out wrong. What she meant was that he would miss *her* season, but he wasn't thinking about that. He laughed abruptly.

'I would be entirely happy if this was the last ballroom I ever set foot in,' he said, a hard edge to his words. Minnie's eyes stung as though he'd hit her, and she looked away, not wanting him to see how much he had upset her.

'Minnie, I didn't mean—,' Eric's voice softened but Minnie couldn't look at him. Her heart was smarting. He hadn't even counted the cost of not seeing her as often.

'Listen Minnie,' he said, laying his hand on hers.

'Eric—oh Eric I'm so glad I've found you,' came the strident tones of Nellie from behind them. 'Are you sure there's no way we can leave earlier than dawn? I'm afraid I've had my fill of amusement from these people. They make rather predictable, dull sport after a while. Oh,' Nellie came to a stop beside them and looked with insincere surprise at Minnie. 'I'm afraid I didn't see you there, Minnie.'

Minnie pulled her hand away from Eric's.

'Eric was just saying how pleased he would be to leave,' said Minnie, her voice brittle, the lump in her throat cutting off all warmth to her voice. 'I'm sure we can find one of the villagers to row you back, although goodness knows when the next train will be.'

'Minnie,' said Eric, his voice low.

She saw him reach out to her, but she turned away.

'If you'll excuse me, I should be getting back. Supper must nearly be over.'

CHAPTER 3

As dawn broke over Widuwe, the guests trod wearily down the path to the pier where a fleet of little fishing boats waited to carry them back to the mainland. The boats were all stocked with thermoses filled with coffee and a basket of pancakes to keep everyone warm and full during the trip back.

With her parents and Jack occupied with farewelling the guests, Minnie slipped away and climbed the southern bluff to find refuge for her aching heart under the old oak tree.

But when she came out of the woodland that covered the climb to the bluff, she saw that she was not alone in looking for solitude.

Eric was standing by the edge of the bluff, looking handsome in his tails as he looked out over the ocean and the gentle, morning sky.

Minnie paused, unsure if she had it in her to withstand another snub from him. But he turned and reached out a hand to her, a look of such contrition on his face that her reserve melted.

'I hoped you would come up to see the dawn,' he said, his

grey eyes smiling at her, the worry chased from his face by the wonder of the sunrise.

The wings in her chest fluttered as she looked into his eyes, the tension of the previous night evaporated and they were Eric and Minnie again, companions of old. Minnie gave Eric her hand and sighed softly as she looked over the dawn-soaked morning. This had always been Minnie's favourite spot. She liked the feel of Widuwe behind her, the curve of the mainland reaching out to embrace their little island in a safe, shallow bay, the wild uncertain stretch of ocean before them.

'You were waiting for me?' she asked. He nodded, not taking his eyes from her, and the hummingbird in her chest stirred. She stood beside him, but even as he smiled at her, the shadows were gathering in his eyes again.

'I wanted to apologise,' he said, 'and to explain. Nell can be a bit—abrupt.'

Minnie thought that there were more fitting adjectives for the forthright Miss Radcliffe, but she held her peace. Eric let go of her hand and turned his back on the view to look at her fully.

'I learned something about my father recently,' he said.

Minnie frowned up at Eric, noticing how the light of the dawn sat golden on his shoulders. He and his father had never been on good terms. It was why Eric had spent so much time at Widuwe rather than at his own family property in the mountains.

From the set of Eric's brow it did not look as though what he had learned had improved things.

'He was a partner of the firm Fink, Best and Phillips. Does that mean anything to you?'

'No,' said Minnie.

'They were the architects of the land boom back in the eighties. He not only profited from the ruin of hundreds of families, he *engineered* it, Minnie. He created the risks and then allowed the crash, all for profit. I didn't even understand the magnitude of what people had lost, until I started visiting some of the poorer areas of the city. And then to find that my *father* was responsible for all that poverty and loss of life—!'

Minnie thought of the stories they had heard as children, of the baby farmers and the piles of dead, neglected infants. The mothers who had been tricked into giving up their children in exchange for a promise of a better chance for them. She pressed her hand to her mouth.

'Do you understand, now, why I have to do this? The money my father made, it made him the important man he is today. It paid for my upbringing, it paid for my education. When I found out, I felt rotten with shame. As though the very fabric of my being was drenched in the stench of corruption.'

'No, Eric. You've never been anything like your father.'

'I'm his son. I've profited from his evil. I tried to quit university then and there, but the dean, Mr Radcliffe, wouldn't hear of it. He pointed out that there was no nobility in starving myself and wasting money that had already been spent on an education that was all but complete. Why not, he said, complete my studies and put them to good use, aiding the very people my father had ruined? So that is what I intend to do. I couldn't work with my uncle, living comfortably, earning good money, knowing that children were going without food because of my family.'

'No,' said Minnie. She looked out at the ocean, at the white tips of the waves that chewed at each other in the distance, over the stretch of water that hid the reef below. She pushed on her top lip, trying to find a way to voice her fears without sounding selfish. It hadn't felt selfish before, but in light of what Eric had told her—

'It's just...' she trailed off, squinting at a fishing boat tugging away from the reef. 'It feels like you're abandoning me, us— everyone. It feels like you're punishing us as well as your father.'

'I'm not punishing Father. I'm trying to atone for his actions.'

'It feels like a punishment,' Minnie muttered.

'Minnie, please, can you try to understand?'

Minnie took her eyes from the ocean and looked up at Eric. There were changes in him that she hadn't noticed before. The lines she had seen, the severity of his look; but she had not seen the new understanding and the awakened compassion in his outlook. She felt a new awareness in herself too, as she looked on his dear, familiar, and yet different face. She felt it in the heat of her cheeks and the heavy shame that stilled the wings of the hummingbird in her chest.

'Yes, I do understand,' she said, dropping her eyes away from his. 'But, oh Eric, it all seems so terribly final. Will you really have nothing to do with any of us anymore? Will you exile yourself all for the sake of honour? Your father was the one to make the mistakes, not you.'

'What's the point of a childhood lived in fairy tales and adventure if we don't grow to be worthy of those values?' Eric asked her. He was smiling, but the earnestness did not leave his eyes.

'Will I not see you anymore?' asked Minnie, her chest feeling hollow, her words desperate.

'I'll be back for Easter, if you'll still have me, but after that, I don't know, Min, when we are likely to see each other again.'

Minnie closed her eyes, refusing to cry in front of him. If, in that moment, he asked her to go with him, she would say yes. But he didn't ask.

'I already thought you worthy,' said Minnie quietly, looking down the slope of the hill that vanished into a cliff. 'You're the most honourable man I know.'

'Ah, but I have not yet been challenged,' said Eric, nudging her with his shoulder. 'If you still think me worthy in a year, that will be an honour indeed.'

~

AND WHAT OF her in a year?

The thought tormented Minnie as she walked with Eric down to the pier where the boats were waiting, picking her way carefully as she held the hem of her gown clear of the sandy track.

The shame that had crept over her at the realisation of her own selfishness in the face of Eric's sacrifice lay slick and dark on her heart. She had wanted a gallant admirer with her in the ballrooms of Melbourne, a man to fall in love with her over the course of a year of gaiety. But Eric was going after true heroism. And she'd had the short-sightedness not only to feel piqued at Eric's denial of her dream, but the idiocy to voice it to him as well. Nellie was right. What would there be for him a year later to cause his thoughts to turn towards her with anything but disdain?

She loved Eric. She had always loved him. She had thought herself in love with him, but was that the truth, or merely a childish romantic wish? Because, she reasoned with herself as they trod in silence down the steep path of the cliff with the waves broiling on the rocks below, if she truly loved him, would she not want to spend the rest of her life with him, no matter what?

But the news of his decision to look away from everything they knew and choose another path filled her with despair. She didn't want to live a life away from her family and friends and the parties she loved and the beautiful clothes she could buy and the comfort her father's money provided. She liked all those things.

Minnie watched Eric climb into one of the waiting boats, her heart heavy, her arms longing to reach out and hold him. The only thing she could be sure about was that the thought of losing Eric was a pain so dreadful, that if it happened, she didn't know how she would survive it.

CHAPTER 4

Good Friday

The train swayed around the bend and a view of Swan Bay opened up before Eric's gaze. At the mouth of the bay sat Widuwe, a calm sentinel in the mass of black water that chewed at its edges. The sky was low and dark and further out over the ocean the clouds bled into the horizon in angry streaks.

The causeway was long under water, and eying the waves that churned hungrily between the mainland and Widuwe, Eric sighed, resigned to an evening of tedium in the village hotel.

He hadn't heard from Minnie since the ball. He'd tried to write, but what was the point? He'd done well in his final exams. He was now, to all intents and purposes, a doctor. It was a hollow triumph. His graduation certificate heralded the end of his dreams where Minnie was concerned. He'd heard the dismay in her tone that dawn up on the bluff. He didn't need her to put into words her horror at the sacrifice which loving him would entail. Because that was what he wanted from her, what he had wanted to give her, where he assumed the year would take them before his discovery about his father had made it all impossible.

The train pulled into the village station and the clouds were thick and black in the sky. In the harbour the fishing boats huddled at their moorings, straining nervously at their anchors. As he climbed out of the train large spatters of rain fell into the dust of the road. Eric put his hat on and got a more secure grip on his suitcase and prepared to make a run for it when he heard his name being called.

He turned and saw a fishermen he'd known since they were boys together, Jem Masters, running towards him, a look of terror on his face.

'Eric, my cousin Jemima's having her baby, and the doctor's out of town and trapped by the storm.'

Eric put his suitcase down and put a hand on the shoulder of the frightened young man.

'Jem, take a breath mate. Where's the midwife?'

'The doctor went to fetch her, but Sweeney's Track has been washed out and they're trapped up in the hills.'

Eric frowned. 'Why is there no midwife in the village? Well, never mind that now. Of course I'll come and do what I can to help. I must warn you, I've only recently finished my exams and have next to no experience, but I suppose I'll be better than nothing.'

'I'm heading to the island, I'm on my way to get Miss Minnie.'

'Are you mad, Jem? You can't take Miss Wyndam across in this weather,' said Eric.

'I have to, Eric, Jemima's asking for her, and she's so scared, I'm afraid what will happen if I don't get her. Miss Minnie would want to know.'

'Jem, you'll be drowned. Look at the ocean.'

'There was a time you trusted me on the water, sir.'

The two men looked at each other and Eric felt the companionship of their youth beat underneath his fears. He sighed and shook his head.

'You'll take the self-righting boat? And make her wear a life jacket?'

'I will.'

'Alright, take me to your Jemima and then you can go across to Widuwe.'

Why on earth Jemima wanted Minnie, let alone thought she would be of any practical assistance right now was a mystery to him. But he knew Jem, and trusted his instinct, so he followed him out into the rain and hurried along behind him into the flats that housed the fishermen and their wives.

CHAPTER 5

In the main room of a small wooden cottage, Jem's cousin Jemima was standing bent over a chair back, her night dress clinging to her with sweat despite the chill of the room. Her husband Sam stood by her head, alternatively stroking her hair and patting her back, her face white and drawn.

'How long has she been labouring for?' Eric asked Sam quietly.

'Since this morning,' said Sam. 'She was fine when she started, much calmer than I expected, and we knew the doctor would be back by dinner time with the midwife. But then the storm started, and the roads were washed out and when the wind started howling, the fear set in, and she started shutting down. Everything has slowed up, except the pain.'

'Why is it so cold in here?'

'We've run out of wood. She wouldn't let me leave her to cut any more.'

Eric, after getting Jemima's permission, conducted a brief examination.

'Your baby's doing well,' he informed the anxious parents. Sam nodded with relief, but Jemima didn't answer. Her face was drawn and pale, and her eyes were closed as she rocked back and forth, murmuring to herself.

'Is Miss Minnie coming?' asked Sam anxiously.

'Jem's gone across in his boat to fetch her,' said Eric, his jaw tightening at the thought of Minnie in the rough sea. 'Tell me, why does Jemima need Miss Wyndam here?'

Sam looked down at his wife, who showed no sign of paying any attention to them. He shrugged. 'It's a female thing,' he said. 'Jemima worked as a maid over at the big house before we were married. Miss Minnie has been keeping an eye on Jemima since we discovered about the baby. She knows Jemima frets when I'm out in the boat and she's here on her own.' Sam paused, frowning over his thoughts. He shook his head. 'I dunno what it is about Miss Minnie, but she's the only one as can keep Jemima calm when she's getting in a state about the baby.'

MINNIE DID NOT THINK she would forget the boat ride from Widuwe for as long as she lived. The storm, which had been gathering its forces as they left the house, blew into itself as they reached the jetty. With the blackness of the night and the rain driving across her face, Minnie could hear more than see the ferocity of the waves. They clambered aboard Jem's broad-bottomed self-righting boat and Jem grabbed a pair of oars and pulled towards the mainland. They were on the leeward side of the island, where the water was less fierce and the winds tempered by the bulk of the island, but even still it was hard going.

Minnie concentrated on holding on for dear life and remembering everything she knew to be true about the marvellous technology of the self-righting boats. More than once a wave tried to engulf them, breaching the sides of the boat so that the water covered them and swirled around their feet and calves. They could not talk to each other, but every time a wave soaked them Jem would cry out with a reassuring 'Hi-Hum!' that somehow gave heart to Minnie, feeling small and cold and insignificant in the middle of the hungry sea.

Soon they pulled in alongside the jetty with a violent thump, and with as much haste as they could manage with their frozen limbs, clambered out of the boat and ran through the howling rain and muddy streets to the cottage in the flats.

They crept in quietly through the kitchen door, trying their best not to make any noises to disturb Jemima. They stood by the stove, shaking the rain from them and peeling off their wet overcoats. The door to the inner room opened and Eric appeared.

'Minnie, thank God you made it safely,' he said, striding towards her with outstretched hands. All the reserve of their previous meeting was gone and Minnie felt some of the tension leave her shoulders.

'It was certainly quite a journey,' she said, letting him take her hands in his. Her heart grew warm in her chest.

'You're frozen—!' he exclaimed, feeling her hands.

'Never mind about that, I'll soon thaw. How is Jemima?'

Eric frowned, looking down at her.

'Physically, she's fine. But she's terribly frightened and it's slowing everything down.'

'Is she in any danger?' Minnie asked, the ice from her hands sneaking its way into her veins.

'Not at present, but if it goes on too long there is a risk of infection to mother and baby.'

Minnie bit her lip and nodded, thinking hard.

'If we could get her to relax?' she asked, looking up into Eric's face. He was watching her intently and she felt a stirring in her chest.

'If, and it's a big if, things should progress quite quickly.'

Minnie nodded and squeezed Eric's hands before letting them go.

'You go back to Jemima. I need to fetch something from her room, then I'll join you and see if together we can't make her more comfortable.'

MINNIE ENTERED the main room of the cottage several minutes later holding a picture of the Madonna and Child. She'd noticed the Battista Salvi print the previous Sunday when Jemima had shown off the cot Sam had built for their little baby. Moving quietly, Minnie sat it on the mantle above the fireplace and lit several large candles beside it.

'I need Jemima to be distracted for a time so Sam can go out and cut some more wood,' Eric whispered, coming to stand beside her.

'Jem's gone out to do it,' she whispered back, smiling at him. 'He'd already noticed how low they were.'

'Thank God for Jem,' Eric looked at her for a moment, his eyes dark. 'I couldn't have trusted anyone else to bring you across that water tonight, but Min, I'm extremely glad you came.'

'Of course,' she said, treasuring the humming that started again in her heart. 'I promised Jemima most faithfully to be here if she needed anything.'

Eric gave her a long look, but then behind them Jemima started to whimper and Minnie turned to the poor, frightened girl. Sam was standing by Jemima, who was now kneeling over the back of an armchair, rubbing her back, looking tired and scared. Minnie knelt by Jemima's head and took hold of Jemima's cold hands and started chafing them between her own.

'Would you not like to lie down and rest a while, Jemima?' she asked, massaging the cold fingers and speaking softly.

'No,' said Jemima, her words coming out through grit teeth.

'It would be well for her and the baby if she had a rest,' said Eric quietly. 'The labour's stalled and she'll become too exhausted to birth at this rate.'

'I will not lie down,' said Jemima, more forcefully. 'I won't make the same mistakes as me mam.'

Eric opened his mouth to protest but Minnie hushed him with a look.

'Most sensible,' said Minnie quietly. 'Let's get you resting all the same, without lying down. Eric can fetch the pillows from the bed.'

Eric gave Minnie a frowning look but did as she asked. With the help of the pillows and the heavy quilt from Jemima and Sam's bed and a cushion they made a nest of sorts for Jemima where she could lie her head on the armchair while kneeling on the floor. Minnie spoke quietly to Jemima the whole time she was settling her, placing a towel between her legs and then wrapping her in the thick folds of the quilt and stroking her tired, drawn face. Eric frowned as he watched but did not say anything. Finally, when she was warmer, her hips resting on the pillows Minnie had banked up around her, Jemima's eyes closed and her breathing became more regular. Minnie stayed by her head, stroking her hair and humming softly.

'Well done,' Eric breathed quietly. 'If she can rest sufficiently, then the baby will have an easier time making its way out. If she is as afraid as you suggest then we could be in for a very long, anxious night. Fear is no friend to childbirth.'

Jem came in with an armful of logs and he and Sam set to work building up the fire. The smell of eucalyptus soon filled the room and Jemima stirred.

'Sam—!' she called out, and he hurried to her side, a wild-eyed look in Eric's direction.

Minnie ceded her place by Jemima's head and stood back in the shadows with Eric.

'What happens now?' she asked, her words barely a whisper.

Eric tugged at his ear thoughtfully. 'I know what *should* happen. What will happen is anyone's guess.'

THE STORM WHIPPED itself into an even greater fury. Jemima was breathing heavily, protesting the contractions with low moans. Eric stayed close by, where he could reassure both Sam and Jemima but did not touch Jemima above putting the occasional hand on her belly.

Minnie kept moving between the kitchen and the living room, keeping a supply of hot towels at the ready. The walls of the little cottage shook as the wind ripped through the street. The iron roof groaned and Jemima panted, her face covered in sweat. She was standing again, her arms wrapped around Sam who patted her hair, silent tears wet on his cheeks. Eric spoke quietly, his voice calm, but his jaw was set and his eyes were strained.

Jemima moaned again, and the sound grew and sharpened. She cried out, pain and fear cutting through the rage of the storm.

'Mama—!' Jemima screamed. 'I can't, I can't do it.' Her scream settled into a sob and she hung off Sam's neck, great heaving sobs shaking her thin shoulders.

'For pity's sake!' Sam looked wide-eyed at Eric who had his hands on Jemima's tight belly. 'Can't you end it?'

'It's up to the mother and the child, and they are doing splendidly,' said Eric. Minnie saw how worried he was but Sam seemed to take some comfort from his words.

Eric stood back from the couple as another contraction started and Jemima's screams started again.

'She's so frightened, there's not enough room for the baby to descend,' said Eric to Minnie in a low voice.

'Is the baby stuck? Is that dangerous?'

'If it goes on for too long it can become dangerous. We could encourage the baby to move, but she's too frightened to try anything. I think she's convinced herself that she is going to die, like her mother, and if she can't talk herself out of that thought, she may well.'

'Oh Eric,' Minnie's heart tightened and her eyes were awash with tears.

'Don't lose hope,' said Eric, grasping her hands in his. 'We are a long way from that yet. You've done so well so far. We can get her through this.'

'Yes, of course. I'm sorry,' said Minnie, brushing her hand over her eyes.

'From my best guess, I would say the baby has his arm around his neck, which is why the contractions are so painful. Every time her body tries to push the baby down, the elbow gets rammed into her tail bone, causing pain and making her fight the contractions. We need to get the baby to shift so that the arm either comes down, or the baby moves past it.'

'How do we do that?' Minnie asked, biting her lip as Jemima started calling for her mother again, her panic slicing the stillness of the room.

'If she could relieve herself, it might help. Otherwise we need her to get her to shift her hips, so that one is lower than the other, change the shape of the pelvic outlet so that the baby has room to move his arm.'

Eric returned to Jemima and Sam, and Minnie slipped back out into the kitchen to look for a chamber pot.

When she had the pot, Minnie sent the men from the room and held Jemima as she relieved herself. When she had finished, before Minnie had a chance to help her back to her nest, Jemima gasped and threw herself on the floor on her hands and knees and cried out in fear.

'Mama—!' and then she said nothing more as the contraction took hold of her, and her body convulsed, her arms and legs shaking.

The contraction passed and Jemima's body sagged and Minnie caught her and held her against her, kneeling in front of her.

'Mama, mama, mama,' whimpered Jemima, her voice no longer sharp, but faint and threadbare.

'Jemima, look,' said Minnie, willing the girl not to give up. 'Can you see?'

Jemima sighed and opened her eyes, looking at Minnie dully.

'Up there,' said Minnie pointing to the picture on the mantle and the candles burning steadily beside it.

'Your mama is here, watching over you, can't you feel her? But you are a mama now too, and your baby needs you. Look at that little child, the way he snuggles into his mother. You are so close Jemima, and your Mama is so, so proud of you.'

Minnie watched Jemima's face as her glassy eyes came to rest on the picture. Her eyes softened and her dry lips moved silently.

'My baby,' said Jemima softly.

'Your baby,' echoed Minnie, tears dripping salty onto her lips. 'You'll be cuddling him soon, you're doing splendidly.'

She felt Jemima start to convulse again and then Sam

tapped her on the shoulder and Minnie stood, and saw Eric looking at her, in the way she sometimes saw him looking at the ocean.

Jemima gave a shuddering moan and Eric turned to her.

'That's the baby coming now,' he said gently, but loud enough for Jemima and Sam to hear. 'You're almost there Jemima.'

Minnie stood and went to the kitchen and gathered more hot towels and stood silently inside the front room as the baby's head, shoulders and then body emerged. She clutched the towels as Eric bent over the child and there came a faint, mewing cry.

'Oh, thank goodness.' Minnie closed her eyes letting the tears flow freely down her cheeks. The baby cried again and she went forward with the towels and handed them to Jemima, who was resting back on Sam, wonder and exhaustion on her face. Jemima roused herself to take the towel, and then bent forwards to take her little boy. She wrapped him deftly and brought him to her chest.

Eric stood and stepped back from the little family and came to stand by Minnie. Jemima and Sam gazed at their son, and the little babe looked up wonderingly into his mother's face, his little pink mouth working. Eric slipped his hand into Minnie's and gave it a squeeze. More tears spilled from her eyes as Eric pulled her into the circle of his arm and she rested her head on his shoulder and listened to their hearts steady together as the storm blew its last outside.

CHAPTER 6

Easter Sunday

innie woke early on Easter Sunday to a pink, fresh dawn smiling at her through her bedroom window. She lay a long, quiet moment, gazing at the sky, her thoughts caught between childhood and womanhood. The adventures and wonder of her childhood had somehow shifted and changed without her being aware of it. And between long dresses and new hairstyles, she'd forgotten magic and hidden treasure and silence.

She got up, weary of rest, and washed and combed the fright out of her hair. She and Eric had arrived back at Widuwe after breakfast on Easter Saturday, to find a house full of guests half inclined to think they'd eloped together. Minnie, her heart full of Eric, wanted no part of the festivities that had been arranged to celebrate the weekend. She wanted only Eric to herself, to know if he still thought that their's was a hopeless case. But between attending to guests and making up for the sleep she had missed on Friday night,

Minnie had barely exchanged two words with him since they'd returned to the island.

Dressed in a cream linen skirt, with a blouse of ninon and lace, and taking care not to disturb the sleeping house, Minnie left her bedroom and crept outside, making for her favourite spot on the bluff, under the oak. The day was fresh and bright and slightly airless as the world caught its breath after the storm. The fishing boats over by the mainland sat listlessly, as though stunned, some with broken masts, some with sails that had come unfurled and now drooped in the stillness of the morning. The storm had exhausted its fury in the early hours of Saturday morning, and settled into a day of weeping rains that still lay wet all about the ground. Minnie picked her way carefully along the stony path, keeping her skirt clear of the damp.

The sun was just deepening the sky from pink to apricot when Minnie climbed up to the bluff and paused and felt the hummingbird beat its wings in her chest once more.

There, under the amber-leafed oak, stood Eric, his back to her, one palm resting on the trunk of the oak, the other shoved deep in the pocket of his cream flannel trousers. He gazed out at the ocean, still now, and painted pale blue and gold by the light of the Easter dawn.

He was waiting for her. The hummingbird left her, flying on joyous wings into the Easter morn, and she climbed slowly up the hill towards Eric, her heart light with hope.

'Hello sleepyhead,' he said, turning to her with a smile from childhood that had grown into something more. She smiled back at him. He reached out and took her hand and they stood there in the light of the sunrise, side by side, watching Easter break over the sleeping world.

'You were magnificent on Friday,' said Eric, as a light breeze ruffled the leaves of the oak and shook the wildflowers in the long grass. 'I couldn't have gotten through that night without you, Minnie.'

'Don't be silly,' said Minnie, suddenly shy again. 'You knew exactly what needed to happen.'

'But I couldn't have made it happen. I couldn't have applied your empathy and understanding.' He looked down at her, a self-conscious smile pulling at his lips. 'I owe you an apology Min, for my behaviour back in February. I was running scared, and I was too obsessed with my fears to see that I wasn't the only one changing. I always thought I would marry you,' Eric's smile grew into something both hopeful and scared. His eyes were warm as they rested on her and Minnie's breath caught in her throat.

'That's why I was so prickly about the decisions I made about breaking with my father. I knew it would make that dream impossible, it was the only thing that nearly broke my resolve. But then,' he hesitated, searching for the words. He smiled at her ruefully, running a hand through his hair. 'You showed me how stupid I was to consider trying to move on without you.'

Minnie felt the hope in her heart swell. 'I love my life Eric,' she said seriously, 'and I've been looking forward to my debut and the season enormously, I'll not deny it. But when I found out that you wouldn't be there to share it with me, much of the joy went out of it. And I found that I could more happily face life as an outcast with you than live in comfort without you.' She hesitated and her eyes stung at the memory of her doubt. 'I wanted to show you that there was some-thing in me worth putting your faith in.'

'Minnie,' said Eric, looking at her seriously. 'I thought you knew how much I loved you?'

'No,' said Minnie, shy again and looking over Eric's shoulder at the golden-edged clouds in the dawn sky.

'Well, I'm telling you now,' said Eric, taking her other

hand in his and stepping closer to her so that his lips were just near hers. 'I've wanted to marry you ever since that ridiculous night when we were kids and we got stranded out on the rock in the rain. And I thought that's just what I would do. But then I found out this terrible thing about my father and realised the path I must take.'

'You could have asked me to join you,' said Minnie, bringing her eyes to his face in a brief moment of bravery.

'I could not,' Eric protested. 'How could I ask such a thing of you, Minnie, when I was not even sure that I myself could face what was to come?'

'You must know that I am strong enough to face anything that you can,' said Minnie, frowning at him.

'That doesn't follow that it would've been right of me to ask you.'

'You're wrong,' said Minnie, finally meeting his eyes. Eric smiled, his eyes darkening as she turned her face up to him.

'I know that now. I know how strong you are, Minnie, but the quiet everyday sacrifice of everything you know and love, the humility of reduced living circumstances, I could not in good conscience ask that of you. But you embraced it all anyway. You stood by your maid when she had no-one else to support her, and you brought a grace to her situation I wouldn't have thought possible. I woke this morning knowing that I could not let another hour go by without asking your forgiveness, and if—,' but here Eric's courage failed and he broke off, his hands tightening on Minnie's.

'And what, Eric?' she prompted leaning closer to him.

'*Could* you marry me, Minnie? Do you think you could bear it?'

'Oh Eric,' Minnie sighed and closed her eyes, 'it is the only thing I could bear. I was so afraid you meant to do without me.'

'I meant to try,' murmured Eric, leaning closer to her and

pressing his forehead against hers, 'but I was doing a miserable job of it.'

He wrapped his arms around her, holding her close and pressed his lips to hers. Minnie, her heart singing out with joy, slid her hands around his waist, under his jacket and clung to him, feeling the wonder of his kiss and tenderness of his touch. When, at length, Eric's kisses grew a little less fierce, she stepped back to look at him, and her heart crumbled with the realisation of all they had just said to each other. His face grew blurry before her eyes and concern creased his forehead.

'What is it?' he asked softly, catching a tear with his thumb.

'I am so very, very happy,' was all she managed, before his lips sought hers again and his hands cradled her face as he kissed her, more gently this time. As the dawn ripened to day around them, and the birds awoke and the sea breeze shook some leaves from the oak, Minnie understood in the tenderness of Eric's kiss the promise of a lifetime of cherishing, sacrifice, and love.

THE END

AN EASTER LILY ON THE SOMME

By Nancy Cunningham

CHAPTER 1

France, May 1916

Ivy sat on a wooden bench just outside the nurses' compound. One hand held a white daisy, the other, a letter.

My Dearest Ivy...

Why did Mrs Jarrod's letters always begin that way? She wasn't a family member, and she wasn't this woman's dearest anything. She gripped her apron with a fist, unable to stop her rising anxiety. Why on earth was Mrs Jarrod writing to her? Her previous letter—condolences on the loss of Ivy's brother, Samuel—were empty platitudes for a boy she barely knew. A shiver travelled across her shoulders as she continued reading.

Dublin. Easter Uprising.

Uprising? She'd heard little of such events. Not unusual, given the casualty clearing station had only recently settled in Amiens. At Easter, a rumour of rebellion had reached her ears, but they were only rumours. So, the Irish Independence movement had crossed the Rubicon.

Arrested. Assaulted. Black and tan soldier.

'Oh, Pa, what were you thinking?'

Ivy's father held sympathies with the Irish republicans, but his last letter omitted mentioning a Dublin trip. Instead, he'd asked her to come home. And she would have, if Sammy hadn't died. Her duty, steady and calm, had been to remain here, for the rest of her brothers: Ian, Hugh and Oliver.

The letter reeked of strong lavender, making her feel faintly nauseous. But it was the words that followed which made her stomach lurch.

Your father is dead. Heart Attack.

The ink on the paper blurred with drops of tears. 'No.' An unexpected sob escaped. She crushed the letter with both hands, the paper digging into her rough palms. Wasn't it enough her family had given one life to the British cause?

'Ivy?' Sister Florence Peters asked from the edge of the compound. 'Ivy, are you alright?'

Turning her face away, Ivy sniffed. She dropped the letter and daisy to the ground. No-one could see her like this.

'Yes. It's nothing… all these spring flowers are making my nose itchy.'

'Corporal Jones was looking for you. Message from the lieutenant-colonel, they're expecting the new doctor in a few days. He wanted to remind you.'

'I hadn't forgotten,' she replied in a flat tone. Ivy would not let her emotions get the better of her, even after such devastating news.

'Wake me if you want to talk later,' Florence said.

In the evening light, Ivy tracked Florence's movements, waiting for her to retreat. Leaning down, she picked up the letter and jammed it into her pocket. No time to grieve. *Always a solution.* Her mother's motto. One couldn't have heaviness of heart when others needed you.

Ivy trod the daisy into the dirt and hurried to the main

medical tent. With each heavy step she catalogued the letters she must write. Ian should be first, if his wife Laura hadn't informed him already. Then Hugh, and last of all Oliver. She dreaded Hugh's reaction. Her nearest brother's temperament, so different to hers, made her wonder whether they were even siblings. One could never settle a rebellious heart.

An ambulance driver sat smoking a cigarette at the front of the tent, and Ivy marched towards him.

'This is a medical facility, Corporal. If you will smoke, do so outside the perimeter of the clearing station.'

The corporal stood, dropped the cigarette and stomped on it with a hobnail boot.

'Yes, Miss—I mean, Nurse.'

'It's *Sister*. Why are you here? Were you dropping off patients? Have you spoken with Sister Phillips?'

'Not dropping off patients, but someone else, Sister. And I'm to take some injured soldiers to the base hospital. Nurse —Sister Phillips told me to wait.' He gave Ivy an awkward toothy smile. 'I think she's forgotten.'

'I doubt that. While we are very busy, we don't forget. Wait here,' she said and looked him up and down. '*I* won't forget.'

The small clearing station still awaited appointment of a Matron, and until then, it was Ivy's responsibility. The large space inside the tent, divided into triage, evacuation and an area for surgery behind more flaps, bustled with activity.

One of the Voluntary Aid Detachment—VAD—nurses on duty struggled to sit an injured man upright.

'Where are the orderlies, Hollers?'

She shrugged, and Ivy glanced around the room. Only two fellow army nursing sisters and three VADs were on duty. Her head turned at the sound of men's laughter coming from the small service yard at the rear. She pushed aside the canvas flap to find three men loitering.

She cleared her throat. Two of the orderlies, sitting on wooden crates, stood immediately.

'Sister O'Halloran, um…'

'Um, what, Corporal Jones? I have an ambulance man waiting. Why are you not on duty?'

'I ah—we were talking to—'

Ivy interrupted.

'Less talking and more working. Miss Hollers needs assistance.'

The two men hurried back into the tent, leaving Ivy facing a stranger. She studied him with a pinched stare. He cut a rakish figure that towered over her. His frame was burly, his eyes disconcertingly dark. Underneath a neat moustache, he wore a smug grin. She frowned and clasped her hands together in front of her.

'I don't know who you are, and I don't care. Put your scrubs on and help the others.'

His grin widened. Ivy pushed her shoulders back further in response, her frown deepening. Wordless, he touched his forehead in a mock salute, grabbed his jacket and hat, and brushed past her into the tent.

Ivy glimpsed the hat's insignia, and pips on his shoulder. *An officer.*

'Oh, dear,' she mouthed and followed him inside.

*M*aurice couldn't wipe the grin off his face. Although he couldn't see her, he could hear the soft footfalls of Sister O'Halloran following. The nurses and orderlies lit lanterns, shadowing figures with a yellow haze against the tent's ceiling.

Flinging his jacket and hat on an empty bed, he reached down to take hold of a stretcher.

'Heave ho, lad,' he said to the orderly and turned to glance at Sister O'Halloran standing a few yards away. She had a grim, determined look on her face and he lifted one brow, his grin returning when her cheeks reddened.

Outside the tent, Captain Roger Beaufort stood next to the ambulance perusing a clipboard. Without looking up, he directed the stretcher bearers, motioning for them to move fast.

'Come on, the sooner we get them loaded the sooner I can finish these rounds and have a bloody drink.'

'I thought I warned you off the scotch, old man,' Maurice said as he stepped backward into the ambulance.

Captain Beaufort looked up from his clipboard. The deep

frown settling on his face immediately softened to one of surprise.

'Fletcher? Well, I never. When did you get here? Weren't expecting you until Tuesday.'

'I got here when I got here, which was about an hour ago when this ambulance delivered me. I hear clearing station fifty-six is where all hoi polloi meets.'

Beaufort snorted.

'Come to join the riffraff? Should have come and found me.'

'I was told you were doing rounds.' He continued backing into the ambulance. 'Don't worry, the orderlies sorted me out. Heard all the gossip about the place. I feel like I know it already.'

Beaufort pointed to the stretcher.

'That's not your job, Maurice.'

Maurice caught Sister O'Halloran's eye as she emerged from the tent.

'They're shorthanded, so helping the good sister out.'

'Where are the other orderlies, Sister?' Beaufort demanded, as Sister O'Halloran's face flushed an attractive shade of pink.

'It's not her fault,' said Maurice.

Beaufort turned his attention to the orderlies.

'Who's supposed to be on duty? Oh, never mind. Go get the damn roster and check who's on it. Anyone not with you who's on that list when you come back, I'll report to the colonel. Or if they're bloody unlucky, I'll have a word with Sergeant Morgan too.'

'Yes, sir,' the orderlies said in unison and left.

Beaufort turned back to Maurice.

'I have to say, it will please the colonel you're here. He's been charging about like a bull. Making the VADs cry left right and centre. I keep saying Rome wasn't built in a day.'

'But now I'm here.'

'And still a smug bastard.' He held out his hand, and
Maurice shook it. 'How the bloody hell are you, Maurice? In
one piece, I see.'

'Just.' *Unlike Peter.*

'If you'll excuse me, sir,' Sister O'Halloran said, 'but that's
all the men.'

'Rightio, you can go, Sister—oh, wait.' He directed his
gaze back to Maurice. 'Where are your bags?'

Maurice pointed to a nearby trunk and a stuffed kit bag.

'I'll have an orderly deliver them. Sister O'Halloran, take
Captain Fletcher to his tent—he'll be bunking with me.'

'Me, sir?'

'I don't see anyone else here, do you, Sister? It's probably
beneath you, I know, but I've got rounds to finish,' Beaufort
said, nodding towards Maurice. 'I'll let you get settled, old
chap, and join you later.'

Maurice shot Sister O'Halloran a friendly glance and
winked.

Her eyes sparked, and she stood straighter.

'If you wouldn't mind following me, Captain Fletcher.'

'Lead on please, Sister.'

They crossed the open compound of the clearing station
and it gave him a chance to scrutinise the woman who'd
given him a dressing-down. Like all the women here, she
wore a long formless dress, but an army nurse's, not a VAD's.
Her nurse's cap struggled to keep a magnitude of strawberry
blonde curls encased in the confines of its austere design.
Despite the volume of her skirt, he could tell she was slight,
with small hands she kept clasped behind her back. Maurice
jogged to walk beside her.

She looked up at him as she continued, her hurried steps
only stopping once they arrived at a series of tents.

'Captain Beaufort's quarters are the third tent on the right, sir. The walkways can be slippery, so please take care.'

'Not going to show me in?'

'Women aren't allowed in the men's quarters, and vice versa. You best familiarise yourself with the rules, sir.'

'Pity, but I'll keep that in mind,' he said mischievously. 'But what if you have an urgent message to deliver?'

'The orderlies do that.'

He stifled a laugh at her officious reply.

'One of my new orderly friends then. I'm sorry I kept Corporal Jones from his work.'

'There are thirty orderlies stationed here. There should be eight orderlies on at all times. And most of them were missing.'

'We should cut them a little slack, don't you think? Hard work takes a toll on the men.'

'Does it now, sir?' Sister O'Halloran replied with a thin smile and a tight voice. 'Of course, I know nothing about hard work.'

Maurice opened his mouth to reply, but he had none for the diminutive nurse with the indignant stare. She made an abrupt turn and marched back across the compound, offering no goodbye. He let out a low chuckle and made his way towards his tent.

CHAPTER 3

*I*f it were a cold night, steam would rise from Ivy's ears.

'Hard work?' she huffed. Some of these men acted as if this were a playground, not a battlefield. She would make her voice heard. Pa always said she had a persuasive manner... she stopped in her tracks and placed a hand over her mouth to stifle a cry.

'This won't—this won't get the better of me,' she whispered before composing herself and recommencing her stride towards the medical tent.

Once inside, Captain Beaufort called to her.

'Is Captain Fletcher settled, Sister?'

'I assume so, sir,' she replied curtly.

Beaufort replied with a hum and looked her up and down. His easy eyes, always perusing the female staff, made her stiffen.

'Hopkins is out of surgery, but not danger,' he said. 'If you could ask the chaplain to sit with him in case... I'm finished for the night.'

Ivy held back her sudden contempt, nodded and sought

the chaplain before her tongue lashed out at the wolfish Beaufort. She found the chaplain speaking with Sister Evelyn Gorman.

'Padre, Captain Beaufort asked if you would sit with Private Hopkins.'

'Oh, Sister O'Halloran I'm glad you're here. We were discussing a situation with the new volunteers,' he said.

Ivy, guessing what would come next, shot Evelyn a despairing glance. How many times had she had to give the young VAD nurses, many who'd lived sheltered lives, the talk about "masculine ways"? But if putting out these petty fires turned her thoughts away from her father and brother, she'd gladly give a lecture to a legion of silly girls.

'Who's the young man?'

'Private Mathers. Trying it on with all who've been within two feet of him. I told you, Ivy—if they only gave us trained army nurses rather than these flibbertigibbet posh ninnies…'

Ivy, well aware of her fellow sisters' ire, nodded in agreement. Many of the army nurses viewed the VADs as "not real nurses". And those fresh from England often needed conditioning before they were of any use. There was little time for featherheads when injured men came in a constant stream.

'I can handle a soldier giving me a slap and tickle, but these whippets turn to jelly. A hand up to my garter won't bother me,' Evelyn said with a laugh.

Ivy, seeing the chaplain's face had turned bright red, gave him a conciliatory nod.

'Perhaps, Padre, with it being Sunday tomorrow, you could throw in a little extra reminder about good behaviour?'

'Ah, yes, I know what to say. I'll talk about resisting the ways of the flesh and maintaining moral fortitude in the face of temptation.'

'Most prudent,' Ivy replied. Waiting for him to leave, she added, 'Private Hopkins…'

'Oh, deary me, yes,' he said and disappeared.

She turned to Evelyn.

'I'll chat with the girls tomorrow. Should I talk with the Private?'

Before Evelyn could reply, the sound of trucks travelled through the tent.

'That doesn't sound good. We'd best hop to it,' Ivy said. Relief fell across her shoulders. A busy mind left no room for sorrowful thoughts.

Captain Beaufort, still on duty, cursed as ambulance men brought in stretchers of injured men fresh from the aid posts.

'There goes my quiet night.' He lifted the battlefield bandages to assess a wound. 'Evans won't be able to handle all these by himself.'

'You—' Ivy snapped at a nurse. 'Go fetch the other sisters and VADs. And you—' she said to an orderly, 'Fetch the colonel.'

'Sister O'Halloran and Sister Gorman, I want you in the operating theatre,' Beaufort said.

Ivy, following Evelyn, barked orders in her wake.

'Remove that man's wet clothing before he goes into shock.' 'Get the private some pain relief.' 'Put a splint on that limb.' 'You—find some O negative donors.'

When the orderlies brought in four stretchers, Ivy looked up from the wash basin.

'We've only three doctors on duty—'

'I'm here to help,' Captain Fletcher said, his head poking through the flaps to the operating theatre.

His grin took over his entire face, setting Ivy's teeth on edge.

'You can scrub up over there, sir.' She continued readying the trays of instruments for the doctors, but cocked her ear when Captain Fletcher spoke.

'What's your name, lad?'

'William Granger, sir.'

'I know the battle phrase you hate most, William.'

'Sir?'

'Fire at will.'

Ivy turned her head and shot the captain a disapproving glance, but the boy started laughing.

'You're funny, sir.'

'I am at that,' he said. Ivy's cheeks warmed from his mocking grin.

She took a place opposite the lieutenant-colonel and his patient.

'Help Captain Fletcher.'

'But Colonel…' He made no reply and waved her aside. 'Yes, sir.'

Ivy took an apprehensive step towards Captain Fletcher and made a faint gasp when she peered down at the boy's face. He appeared the spitting image of her brother, Samuel. But no, that wasn't right—her head must be in a muddle. It wasn't Sammy.

'Sister O'Halloran disapproves of such merriment. What say you, young Will? Have you any good jokes from the front? Maybe a limerick?'

The boy began laughing again. Ivy, momentarily caught by the boy's countenance, tied her mask behind her head and glared at Captain Fletcher. An operating room was no place for such frivolous cheerfulness. She only drew her stare away from the captain when the pain overcame the boy's mirth and he groaned.

'I don't want to die.'

'Captain Fletcher won't let you die, Private,' Ivy said. She wouldn't let Captain Maurice Fletcher and his impertinent grin make a liar out of her.

CHAPTER 4

$\mathcal{M}$aurice threw his bloodied scrubs into a nearby basket.

'It's called gallows humour, Sister O'Halloran. You have heard of it, yes? The best thing I can do for these men is reassure them that everything is normal.'

'But everything isn't normal, is it, sir?' Sister O'Halloran replied as she rubbed her eyes.

He felt as tired as she looked. Twenty hours on his feet and a further seven in an unfamiliar operating theatre had given him a rude introduction to the casualty clearing station. But nothing for which he wasn't prepared. He loved the bustle, unlike the passive waiting in the hospital—a curse for a man whose hands and mind were never idle.

She was right, nothing was normal, but damn it if he wouldn't make it at least appear that way.

'Did I upset you, Sister?'

'Your levity I object to, sir. There wasn't a single injured man who came through that door where you didn't make light of their injuries. Wholly inappropriate.'

He narrowed his gaze. This little sister's solemnity must

have been difficult to maintain amidst laughter from the other doctors and nurses. Even the lieutenant-colonel had more than a few guffaws for him. And a rendition of 'A Long Way to Tipperary' had garnered an icy glance.

'I don't think anyone minded.'

'These men…'

He put his hand up and glimpsed Roger Beaufort watching them.

'Let me do my job, my way. It hasn't failed me yet. And you do yours. I'm sure someone, somewhere appreciates a certain melancholy in your attentions.'

He regretted the insult at its utterance. But in his sudden exhaustion, his previous joviality had abandoned him. There would be plenty of time to change his tone and invoke the ire of Sister O'Halloran in a far more humourous way.

Maurice left and returned to his tent.

'Sister Ivy O'Halloran—a smiling assassin, that one,' Beaufort said as they entered.

'Hardly smiling, Roger.'

'True. But that's only recent.'

'What? You're telling me she has a sense of humour?'

'Not much of one. Too reserved. A bloody good nurse, though. Best in this clearing station. Good at figuring out what you need and when you need it.'

Maurice thought back to the operating theatre. He'd never been more relaxed under pressure. When he needed an instrument, she handed it to him, as though she'd read his mind.

He opened his trunk and found an unopened whiskey bottle buried in amongst layers of clothes. He shook the bottle towards Beaufort.

'Oh, bloody yes please!'

'What's her story?' he asked, handing Beaufort a glass.

Maurice tingled with curiosity about the pint-sized Sister O'Halloran.

'Her brother died a few months back. Young chap. Only eighteen. What little humour she had seems to have evaporated. She's got an English accent, but I gather with a name like O'Halloran she'd have some waspishness.'

'That's a generalisation.' He recalled his Irish grandmother, a gentle woman with an underlying strong will and good humour. 'No—something else. No-nonsense—reserved, as you say.'

'Like most Englishwomen.' Beaufort took a swig. 'Do you fancy her? Because I can tell you, it will be like scaling a castle wall. You'll never breach her defences. You'll be in the trenches for a long bloody time with that one.'

'I'm not here to go courting.'

Although he'd have to say, Sister O'Halloran's fair features were exactly his type. Even if her temperament wasn't.

'Who's talking about courting them? When you've been here a few more weeks, you'll find some VADs are very accommodating.'

Maurice's brow rose. 'Roger, aren't you married?'

'Unfortunately, yes. Never marry, Maurice.' He took the bottle from Maurice's hand and poured another drink. 'Actually, speaking of—what happened to that friend of yours, that chap you served with in Turkey?'

'Which friend? I served with lots of chaps.'

'The one you brought to dinner. My wife took a shine to him. Wilson, was it?'

'Watson, Peter Watson.'

He'd received a letter from Peter's sister two weeks ago. His friend's fate was the only thing preventing his usual humour taking full flight.

'He's dead. Hanged himself.'

'Bloody hell.'

What he and Peter had gone through on the shores of Suvla Bay had brought his friend to ruin and himself to a deep-seated sense of futility. His levity was the only thing that remained.

He wouldn't let a nurse caught up with the rigidity of hospital ways stop his repartee. He tucked away thoughts about Peter and the failed Gallipoli Campaign.

'Tell you what, here's a bet. Twenty pounds says I'll have Sister O'Halloran splitting the sides of that very severe nurse's outfit before autumn.'

'What? You're bloody mad.' Beaufort laughed. 'A month's wages if you can tear down O'Halloran's exterior? Easiest money I'll ever make.'

Maurice drained his glass and lay back on his bunk. Drifting between wake and sleep, Peter's face came to him like a grey shadow. His thoughts shifted to Sister O'Halloran. Although stiff and with little humour, she had snuck up on him. Her tendrils of sombreness and loveliness crept around him like her botanical namesake.

He dozed, and in his dream, he stood at the foot of a castle wall, a sliver of light poking through a loophole window. From it echoed a laugh and a tumble of strawberry blonde curls, like Rapunzel in her prison.

CHAPTER 5

*I*vy sat and wiped the sweat from Private Granger's brow. She gave a polite nod of greeting to Captain Fletcher. To her, his humour was both a frustrating diversion into inappropriate revelry and a break from unending fear. For what lay less than five miles from here was an insidious creeping terror. Her own losses felt small in comparison. Why not give herself over to some degree of merriment then?

'Is he any better?'

Captain Fletcher's addresses to her were brief but polite. On witnessing his exceptional medical capabilities, Ivy reserved final judgement on his character.

She shook her head. Private Granger had taken a fever two days after surgery. On the sixth day, post-op, he fared no better. Since the first moment Ivy had laid eyes on the boy, and despite her training, she had struggled to maintain a stoic outward demeanour. But she couldn't and wouldn't fail these men. She would show no weakness, not when this boy —these men—needed her strength for their recovery.

Captain Fletcher stood over the boy who furled a gripping hand on Ivy's tunic.

'Drunk much today, lad?'

'I've been very thirsty, sir. My back hurts.'

Ivy patted his hand and looked up at Captain Fletcher for his thoughts.

'Keep him off the rum and the brandy, Sister. A bit of whiskey might be alright. And keep him away from the salted pork, I hear the mess chef overdoes it.'

She stiffened despite the curl of a smile on Captain Fletcher's face.

'So, limit fluids and reduce his salt intake until the nephritis passes?'

'You and I understand each other perfectly,' he replied. Captain Fletcher's smile flickered as if a façade. She understood that flutter of lost hope. She was sure she'd worn that same smile a thousand times since arriving in France.

'Do we?'

Stirrings of quiet anger threatened to overcome her. Surely under her care, he'd improve, no matter if Captain Maurice Fletcher threw a hundred morbid jokes or glances of lost hope at her.

'Captain Fletcher, may I have a word with you? In private.'

He shot her a hesitant glance, but nodded and followed her to a quiet part of the medical tent.

'I refuse to believe that there is nothing we can do for him.'

'The boy has an infection, a fever and likely trench nephritis. When it's this bad, there is nothing more we can do.'

'When he overcomes the fever…'

'*If* he recovers, not when. He's had a fever for four days. I'm surprised he's lasted this long. I'm afraid—'

'No.'

Captain Fletcher stood back.

'Sister, you've seen many men die, as have I. What is it about this boy that is any different?'

'He reminds me of… he…' Her lip quivered. 'It's alright for you,' she said, wishing more than anything to level her gaze at the much taller Captain. 'You throw jokes and laugh and order people around. Who dies, who lives, you decide all. You have no right, you have no right to abandon that boy, none whatsoever.'

Captain Fletcher stared at her silently and placed a hand on her upper arm.

'I'm not abandoning him. But there is nothing more medically possible. Sister, you're exhausted. Go back to your quarters. Rest.'

'No. I won't. If he is to die as you imply, mine will be the last face he sees.'

Ivy's mind raced, like Sammy's stupid go-kart at the top of Baxter's hill. Then she remembered where she was, what her duty was. *Courteous compliance.* She looked up at Captain Fletcher.

'I just want him to know I was there for him.'

'Private Granger or someone else?'

Ivy's breath caught. She peered down like a chastened school girl and walked away with small, hurried steps.

Private Granger opened his eyes when Ivy sat and took his hand. Once again, struck by his likeness to Sammy, she let a soft smile unfurl. The fullness in her chest threatened to burst into a sob.

'Do you have brothers or sisters?'

With a grimace, he nodded.

'A sister.'

She glanced up as Captain Fletcher's shadow fell over both of them. He stared at her, unblinking, and sat opposite.

When he gave her a soft smile, a warmth crept up the back of her neck to her cheeks. She wiped aside several fallen tears.

He pressed a handkerchief into her hand and squeezed.

'Here you go, Ivy. Let's see what we can do about making him comfortable. Yes?'

CHAPTER 6

$\mathcal{M}$aurice watched the orderlies move Private Granger's body from the tent. It had taken two days for him to die. Ivy, who'd sat with the lad throughout the night shift, had disappeared. He had tried to help, but he knew it was fruitless. He'd watched her from a distance, memorising every detail of her face. Soft, but as though she had lived a thousand lives.

He'd seen grief before, a human vulnerability exposed for all to see. But never had he felt it so palpable than in her face. When several strands of her strawberry blonde hair fell over her cheek, he'd had a desire to tuck them back under her cap. To tell her all would be fine. Even if it wasn't.

'Are you coming today, sir?' Sister Peters asked.

Shaken from his thoughts, his eyes widened.

'Coming where?'

'The picnic. Organised through St Johns. Don't worry, we're leaving a skeleton staff behind. The transports are loading now. The farmer has promised cheese and fresh milk. How delicious will that be?'

'Very.'

Maurice wasn't sure after the last few days he could take joy from a picnic. But perhaps that was exactly what he needed.

After changing, he made his way to the clearing station gates. Beaufort, already prepped and ready to depart, stood smoking a cigarette.

'This sunshine makes it feel like there isn't even a war on.'

'I wish,' Maurice replied and hopped onto the first of the vehicles laden with clearing station staff.

The farmer and his short cherub-cheeked wife greeted them on their arrival. As the merry group tumbled from the vehicles, an ambulance pulled up behind them. Two orderlies, carrying an urn between them, exited and followed the farmer's wife inside for hot water.

Maurice, surprised to see Ivy exit the ambulance behind them, headed towards her. She'd left her apron behind and her cap too. A light-headedness hit him.

'Sister O'Halloran, I didn't think you were coming.'

A small smile flickered across her face.

'Everyone needs gaiety once in a while, Captain.'

'Some more than most. May I escort you to the picnic?'

Maurice held out his hand and Ivy studied it before taking it in hers and allowing him to guide her from the ambulance.

She looked around.

'We're going as a group, aren't we?'

At seeing her hair shine in the sun, his breath caught in his throat.

'Yes,' he replied with a nervous laugh.

The sky beat with a brilliant blue. Periwinkles, oxlips, and anemones carpeted the field below the slope. He stared at Ivy as she sat on the grass. The colour of the flowers paled compared to the pleasant pink of her cheeks.

After tea and a robust game of cricket with Beaufort and

the orderlies, Maurice found a quiet spot near the babbling brook. He brought out a small sketchbook, filled with drawings of people he knew, of scenes, of plants and landscapes. He picked a nearby violet and began to draw.

'Captain Fletcher.' He looked up to see Ivy. 'I was hoping to find you alone. I'm not disturbing you, am I?'

He dropped the flower, pencil and sketchbook to his side, and shook his head.

'I wanted to apologise. For everything that has happened between us since you arrived. For mistaking you for an orderly. For taking you to task for your cheerfulness. For my outburst about Private Granger. I didn't mean to question your work ethics and I know you did all you could for him.'

He huffed out a breath. 'I think we got off on the wrong foot. Shall we start our dance again?'

'Sir?'

'I am Captain Maurice Fletcher. I'm Australian by birth. I've three sisters and a dog who I miss very much. The dog that is…' He paused, gave a low laugh and leaned down to pick up his sketchbook. 'And I like to draw.'

Ivy bit her lip and laughed. He liked the sound of that laugh.

'I am Sister Ivy O'Halloran. I'm Irish by birth. I have four brothers.' He caught a sudden shine in her eyes. '*Had* four brothers. And I like to dance.'

She held her hand out to him and he took it in his. Small, comforting and warm from the sun.

'Very pleased to meet you, Sister Ivy O'Halloran. One day, we may get our dance.'

Her face flushed and when he relinquished her hand from his grasp, she tilted her head.

'May I see your drawings, sir?'

Nodding, he handed the battered sketchbook to her. She smiled as she flicked through the pages. Pausing, she frowned, and he leaned forward to see where she had stopped. Her finger traced a drawing of an Easter lily from months ago. In the dull surrounds of a nearby field, the lily's brightness had struck him like lightning. Later he had shaded the drawing pink with pastels.

She looked up at him and the shine in her eyes had turned to tears.

'Aren't lilies white?'

'Usually. But not where I'm from. You don't like Easter lilies, Sister?'

'I like them, yes, very much. It's just that… they remind me of my father.'

He patted the space beside him and swore that his heart doubled in size when she sat close.

'Why don't you tell me about him?'

CHAPTER 7

'We're on leave. Let's not argue, Hugh,' Ivy said and gripped his hand.

'I only asked you to go home. But alright,' he said, then nodded towards the next table and laughed. 'I don't think they believe I'm your brother.'

Ivy regarded the frowning older mesdames.

'I don't care. We look alike, that should be enough.'

Hugh's nose and his colouring, noteworthy O'Halloran features, easily placed them as siblings. The only difference was the subjugation of his strawberry blonde curls by a severe army haircut.

'I miss Sammy and Pa,' he said forlornly. 'I should have been with Pa in Dublin. What the British...'

Ivy placed a finger to her lips. 'Shush, someone might hear you.'

'Pa wrote to me before he went to Ireland. He told me he wasn't going to tell you because you would have stopped him.'

'I would have, yes.'

If only Mrs Jarrod had told her he had a weak heart, like she had gossiped about countless other trivialities. She glanced towards a nearby group of older men in uniform.

'I would like to slap the woman who gave Sammy that white feather. He would never have come…'

'You couldn't stop him. Just as Pa couldn't make you come home.'

'I know.' In her heart, she'd wished her father had tried with Sammy. Boys his age thought they were invincible.

Hugh took hold of her hand, a tight grimace on his face.

'Please Ivy, I'll ask one more time. Go home. Stay with Ian's wife. Nurse at home. They need people like you. It would be a great comfort to me to know you're safe.'

'You're still calling her "Ian's wife"?' she said and chuckled. But how could she sit in that big old comfortable house knowing that he, Ian, and Oliver still fought? 'You know I can't. You know I won't.'

'Then promise me you'll leave if there's danger. Promise me, Ivy.'

Ivy stared at Hugh's wrinkled brow.

'Silly boy. I'm far from the front.'

'Close enough.' He lowered his voice. 'The French have taken heavy losses. There's a big push coming. We could win or lose the war with a single battle. Have you someone at the clearing station who will look out for you?'

Ivy's thoughts veered towards the one person she'd given more thought to than anyone else these past two months. The one person she'd unburdened herself to, about her father and brother. She'd allowed his cheer and good humour to creep into her heart. The twinkle in Maurice's dark brown eyes and the flash of his smile beneath his moustache came to her.

'Sister O'Halloran. Fancy meeting you here,' Maurice said, a large grin on his face.

'Captain Fletcher?' Ivy looked up at the figure standing by their table. 'I didn't realise you'd come to Paris...'

'I had planned to go back to Blighty,' he said and looked at Hugh. 'But I changed my mind.'

Her face flushed.

'Oh, this is my brother, Hugh. Hugh, this is Captain Fletcher. One of the doctors at the clearing station.'

'Pleased to meet you, Captain.'

He shook Hugh's hand and his gaze drifted back to Ivy.

'I can see the likeness. Please, don't let me interrupt your family reunion.'

'No fear of that, sir. Ivy is sick of me hounding her to go home.' Hugh looked at his watch. 'I have to go. Perhaps, sir, if you're headed back to the hospital, you could escort Ivy?'

Ivy's heart fluttered with Maurice's smile.

'I'd be delighted.'

She said goodbye to Hugh, promised she would be careful, and with a nod, took Maurice's arm. They crossed the Seine in silence and Ivy stared up at the Eiffel Tower looming in the distance.

'I hear we have a new matron. I'm surprised the Colonel didn't choose you.'

'He probably thinks I'm too young.'

'I forgot—most army matrons are battle axes. Well-worn with age and use.' He stared down at her. 'Don't let war make you taciturn, Sister.'

'I fear it's not war per se that makes me taciturn. It's the futility of it.'

'I feel the same.' He gripped her arm tighter. 'I hope you won't think ill of me, but although I serve King and country, I can't help but feel deceived by Australia's alliance with

England. After what happened in Turkey… the death of so many.'

'Your friend Peter?'

When Maurice had talked of Peter, it was always with veneration.

'The futility of war has been my constant companion of late.'

Ivy halted in her tracks. In a brief amount of time she'd understood his irreverence. His humour—a mask, one born of discontent much in the same way as her standoffishness. The very army they served had betrayed them both.

'I've lived in England since I was very young, but I still feel Irish in my heart. My father's death has shaken my loyalties to the British. And I worry about Hugh. He's angry. As am I.' She gave a small laugh. 'I'm sure what we say is treasonous.'

He drew her closer and cupped her cheek with his hand. She'd always thought him handsome, but, now, up close, more so than ever.

'Then let us go to the gallows together.'

Before she knew it, she was kissing him. A deep defiant kiss. Irrational, illogical, and everything she'd fought against since she'd met him. She felt his moustache tickle her upper lip and his hands grip her waist tight. The kiss made her heart swell. Her emptiness filled with mischievous euphoria. And for as long as his lips remained pressed against hers, sorrow, pain and anger dissolved into joy.

CHAPTER 8

July 1, 1916

'Did you enjoy the celebrations, Matron?'

Maurice handed her the final list of medicines needed for the day.

'I'm afraid the cake gave me heartburn, Captain.'

'That's why you take the candles off first,' he said with a grin.

Matron Ferrier's laugh carried through the supply room, deep and hearty. Not so much battle-axe as he'd first expected, instead, a competent yet jovial personality carrying wit along with reason. Someone with a view on life like his own.

'Captain Fletcher, you are a distraction,' she said.

'It's the least I can do, Matron,' he replied and tried to catch Ivy's attention with an impish glance.

She ignored him and continued taking an inventory of bandages and dressings. Despite a passionate embrace on the banks of the Seine, Ivy had retreated. Not that there had been time for any indiscretions. In their devotion to their duties, they had laid passion aside.

The Matron disappeared out the door leaving them alone. Maurice sidled up beside the preoccupied Ivy.

'My sweet lily, may I have a kiss?' he whispered into her ear.

She gave him a tight-lipped smile and pecked him on the cheek.

'There you go.'

'No, no, no.'

Taking the clipboard from her hand, he placed it on the nearby shelf and drew her into his arms. He silenced her objections with a kiss, one she melted into with a willing softness that made him release a small groan. Relief that her passion remained, he relished how blissful he felt when he held her, his need for her overcoming all wisdom.

She pushed against him.

'We can't do this, Maurice. Not here. Someone will see us.'

'Let's talk about it then.'

'We don't have time.'

He hadn't wanted to compromise her, for if caught, her punishment would exceed his. Despite the fire for her burning in his gut, he had to put his own selfish need for her aside. Releasing her from his grasp he stood back just as the Matron re-entered the supply room.

'Finished yet, Sister?'

Ivy, red cheeked, gave her a wavering smile and handed her the clipboard.

'We're down on bed dressings and rolled bandages.'

'The volunteers have been boiling and re-rolling bandages for hours. Go light a fire under them.'

'Yes, Matron,' Ivy replied.

Maurice's gaze followed her as she left and he returned to a stock-take of the medicine cabinet. When he finished, he shut the glass door, locked it with a key and handed it over to Matron. She stared at him with a gaunt smile, one that made him feel like a misbehaving school boy.

'Sister O'Halloran is very efficient.'

'Yes,' he replied. Matron Ferrier had to be hinting at something. Had she seen him steal a kiss from Ivy?

'I knew her and her family before the war, did she ever mention that?'

'No, she didn't. No time to chit chat.'

'Yes, well, not that it's appropriate for doctors to fraternise with the nursing staff. Goodness knows, in the time I've been here, I've had to warn off Captain Beaufort and send one perfectly good VAD home.'

'I heard.'

'I like you Captain.' She looked him up and down. 'In these times, we are all prone to emotional liability, and seeking comfort from others is only natural. But I wouldn't wish to *expose* my nursing staff.'

'I'm not sure what you mean, Matron.'

'Oh, I am certain you do,' she said, smiled, patted his shoulder and left.

Maurice drummed his fingers on a nearby wall. He needed to talk with Ivy—now. Before he could leave, a VAD nurse rushed in.

'Captain, we have casualties,' she said on the verge of tears. 'Hundreds of them, I've never seen so many before.'

He answered with a frustrated nod. His conversation with Ivy would have to wait.

CHAPTER 9

$\mathcal{I}$n all Ivy's nursing years, exhaustion had never come quite like this. The heated battle along the front drew numerous casualties, and the brutal beginnings of the Somme Offensive had killed one of their own.

Matron Ferrier was dead, killed by mortar fire just outside the clearing station perimeter. An army reaped what they sowed. Thoughts of her own safety felt selfish, especially when so many were willing to put themselves in the line of fire.

Ivy's hands clenched at her sides.

'We're overrun with injured and dying. We're low on supplies. Not to mention demands from brigades passing through to the front. Unless supplies are replenished, more men will die, Colonel.'

'You don't think I know that, Sister? The doctors have already told me, more than once. Even Captain Fletcher's good humour has left him.' He pointed to Maurice.

Ivy wanted nothing more than to close the space between her and Maurice. Calmed by their connection and her growing affection for him, her familial grief had returned with Matron's death and with each man who died in her care. Underneath she longed for his touch and mourned its waning. But duty called—to them both.

Maurice interrupted her thoughts.

'We can't handle this many casualties. We're at a breaking point. Brigadier—'

The Colonel cut him off. 'I don't want to hear about Brigadier-General Morrow.'

Besides the casualties, the echo of guns closing in on them meant more infantry and artillery men heading to the front. And along with them—their imperious leaders. In three weeks, almost six thousand wounded men had passed through the gates. At twice their capacity the casualty clearing station had also lost two staff.

'You'll just have to make do. Dismissed.'

Maurice tapped Ivy's arm.

'Sister O'Halloran, a word outside.'

She followed him out to the porch of the colonel's quarters.

'What is it?'

'We've not had a chance to talk.'

'If you haven't noticed, we're inundated.'

Ivy turned to leave, but he put a hand on her shoulder.

'The brigadier plans to make all the women leave.'

'What? But he can't do that! The Colonel will be furious. The clearing station needs nurses and—'

'It was my suggestion. The colonel thinks this is still a clearing station. But it isn't. It's a battlefield triage unit now, and it's no place for women. Morrow will tell him soon enough.'

His suggestion? The Brigadier's arrival signalled a change. But Maurice had known how hard she'd fought to remain here.

'Matron didn't give her life so they could send us back.'

'What would it matter to you if you are here or at the base hospital or even back in Blighty? It's too dangerous here. The other doctors and I agree.'

Faced with danger, he was like every other man she'd met. Women were nothing but pawns to move around. She thought back to the expectations of the British army hierarchy: men were to be brave, show courage, energy and patience. From women they expected loyalty, humility and above all—obedience.

'I can be all the things men are. Generous, brave. Yet where they warn men off French wine and loose women, I am warned not to step out of bounds. But all I wish for with all my heart is to put my life on the line like my brothers.' She would not leave. 'No-one consulted us nurses. Why should these decisions be only the domain of men?'

He let out an exasperated sigh.

'You're a distraction, Sister O'Halloran.'

'Like your humour? I'm afraid unlike your drollness, in a medical setting I actually have some practical use.' *A distraction.* 'I'm going to tell the colonel he needs to know...'

He grabbed her arm. She tried to shrug him off, but his grip was like iron.

'It doesn't matter what you tell the colonel. You'll all be gone within a day. Ivy, I had hoped if we couldn't be...' Maurice's crimson cheeks stood out against his dark moustache. 'I had hoped you might still consider me a friend.'

'A friend? This is war, Captain Fletcher. And like those men in the trenches, I don't need friends. I need people to believe in me.' *And he didn't.* 'Now please let me go.'

His hand dropped to his side, and an unreadable expression crossed his face. He strode away without reply, leaving her empty and without breath. How did she end up here?

How could *she* become so diverted and allow him to sweep her off her feet like a whirlwind? *A distraction?*

She laid her head against the door, fighting the weakness that threatened to invade her limbs.

'Bring the next one in,' Maurice said. He looked down at the patient as they transferred him from a stretcher to the operating table. The man's wounds had penetrated deep and he could do little beyond surface dressing. When he had finished, he let out a frustrated sigh.

'Take this man to recovery. Make him comfortable.'

What he wouldn't give to be diagnosing a less noble disease of immoral excess than these wounds tearing men apart.

'That's all there is for now, sir,' the orderly said. 'The Colonel's asking for help in the main tent.'

He uttered a *thank god* and hobbled to a nearby bench. Someone passed him a flask of water and asked if he wished for food. He shook his head, downed all the water in his flask before putting on a fresh set of scrubs.

In the recovery tent, a sea of men's faces greeted him—no Ivy. Maybe he'd made a mistake, to take off his armour in front of her, let her see a glimpse of the man underneath. He leaned over a gassed patient struggling to pull a blanket over himself and pulled it up to the man's shoulders.

'Have all the nurses left?' he asked a passing orderly.

'They're loading the last lot of patients. The nurses are going with them.' He pointed towards the tent exit. 'They're gathering at the gates, sir.'

He stood, surveying the injured and dying. If love were light, it was now missing its brightest star. *No—Not a mistake.* He ripped off the gown he'd put on only moments before and dashed to his tent.

He found his sketchbook, ripped a page from it and wrote on the blank areas surrounding the drawing. Stuffing it into an envelope and his pocket he sprinted to the gates. Nurses and orderlies, engaged in nervous chatter, loaded wounded and bags into trucks. He looked around at all the faces he'd come to know well. Only one face was missing.

From across the compound the colonel and brigadier approached. Ivy marched between them, dwarfed by the men's height and looking like their prisoner. He took her bag from her before she could object and heaved it in with the others.

'Captain Fletcher,' she said and waited until the colonel and brigadier were out of earshot before continuing. 'I suppose you're satisfied to have your way.'

'It's not about getting my way, you know that.'

'Isn't it?' Ivy let out a frustrated harrumph. 'You're exactly like every other man I know. You want me to bend to your will. If I don't listen to the men I care…' She paused, her face reddening. 'If I don't listen to my brothers, why would I listen to you?'

'Because I am a senior officer. I'm not asking you to stop what you're doing, you do it very well. The men you save will never know how lucky they are to have had you nurse them.'

'You said I was a distraction. Is that a personal declaration? Am I a distraction to you and your duties?'

He didn't know how to answer that. His head was full of

her. But if he were to keep her safe, to keep her mind occupied of thoughts other than of him, he had to lie about his feelings for her. The note would explain everything, and he hoped she would forgive him.

'No. Never.'

Her expression fell at his words. He wanted nothing more than to hold her then, but she turned and took an orderly's hand and hoisted herself into the back of the truck.

He came closer to her, the noise of the engine threatening to drown him out.

'This is a cataclysm we're both caught in. Perhaps you think our closeness was in error?'

Ivy spoke without looking at him.

'I don't know what you mean, Captain. I am barely acquainted with you.' She turned and delivered an empty stare his way. 'Good luck to you, sir.'

The truck pulled away. In his heart he wanted to say sorry, that he believed in her more than he believed in himself.

His last glimpse of her was a futile grimace before she looked away.

~

November 1916

'COME ON, old chap. You can't keep it up, you know. You've completely lost your good humour since the—what is it you Australians call them? Sheilas isn't it?' Beaufort didn't wait for Maurice to answer. 'Yes, since the sheilas left.'

Maurice gave a quiet laugh and thumped his leg with a closed fist. Over three months had passed since the brigadier-general made the nurses and Ivy leave the clearing station. Since then—not a single word from her. *She must hate him.*

Beaufort tossed him an almost empty bottle. 'Sleep your moroseness off, man. I have to get back to it.'

He gave a disinterested hum in reply. When Beaufort left, he uncapped the bottle and drained the remaining liquor. He lay back on his bunk, a light pattering of rain sounding against the roof of the tent.

A faint whistling accompanied an increase in the rain, and Maurice cocked his ear to the sound. A violent noise cracked the surrounds. The tent collapsed around him causing confusion. Smoke swirled and an acrid smell made him reel. When he touched his temple, his fingers came away wet and thick with a consistency he knew well—blood.

CHAPTER 11

*W*ith months of the Somme Offensive behind them, the base hospital, four times the size of the clearing station, remained busy. Since her arrival, she'd had little time to ruminate on what had happened between her and Maurice. But did it matter? He'd made it clear how he regarded her and pushed her away.

Although every day she gave herself over to thoughts of what could have been, other events had occupied her mind too. Her father's estate remained unsettled, and Hugh—now at home and recovering from serious injury—meant her burden was twofold. Her duty now split between here *and* home. She'd only just begun a letter to Hugh when Florence dashed into their shared room.

'Oh, Ivy! You're here!'

'Flo, I thought you'd left to go dancing?' She'd not been in the mood to join her friend. 'What's got you all in a flap?'

'I almost forgot. I was sorting through my things this morning and I found this—' Florence retrieved an envelope from her bedside drawer and handed it to her. 'It's been in my bag for an age but I didn't see it. He must have put it in the wrong one. I have to go. Tell me all about it later!'

Ivy, confused, turned the envelope in her hand as Florence dashed out the door. Inside the envelope was a page from Maurice's sketchbook. The pink Easter lily. And in the spaces between, words written in a hasty hand.

Please forgive me. I pushed you away to keep you safe. I know most Easter lilies are white and mean hope. But to me the pink ones are special. You are my pink Easter lily. You are my hope. Ivy, I believe in you. I love you.

Maurice xx

She gasped and dropped the letter. 'You stupid, stupid, man.'

Picking up the message, she read the words over again and laid a hand on her heart. The tears she had held back for so long, for her brother, her father and Maurice, flowed unimpeded. Since she left, her emotions had rolled like waves, peaks and troughs of compassion, surprise, anxiety, anger, and despair. But hope had remained through it all, buried under the deluge. He had pushed her away, not because he didn't have faith in her, but because he loved her. *He loved her.* She closed her eyes, remembering every kiss, every touch, every stupid joke he'd ever told.

When her crying subsided, she wiped her face on her sleeve and scribbled a note to him. Why delay or deny it any longer? She loved him and couldn't remember not loving him.

Intending to find a driver heading for the clearing station, she left her quarters. Making a mad dash through the busy building, she collided with a soldier. She looked up to see a familiar face.

'Corporal Jones, what are you doing here?'

'They evacuated us, Sister. The Germans are trying one last push by trying to bomb us back to Blighty,' he said and grinned. 'But we've got them on the hop. A bunch of frightened bunnies in Lederhosen.'

'Evacuated?' Ivy's heart thumped. 'You mean everyone is here? Including the doctors?'

'I think so. I'm to return to fetch the last lot of stragglers… but…'

She didn't wait for him to finish and raced through to the triage area. Seeing soldiers and orderlies from the clearing station made her burst into a happy sob. She stopped dead in her tracks when a man in front of her groaned.

'Captain Beaufort…'

His gaze wavered.

'Sister O'Halloran?'

She knelt next to him.

'Is Captain Fletcher with you, sir?'

'No…' He grabbed her arm. 'The Colonel—he's dead.'

A growing panic made her heart beat wildly.

'It will be alright, sir,' she said, perused his injuries and called for a VAD nurse. 'I have to go, but I'll be back, I promise.'

No Maurice amongst the evacuees. There was only one thing she could do. Darting in and around the trucks, horse and carts and the many ambulances unloading in the hospital compound, she spotted Corporal Jones and jumped into the ambulance's passenger side beside him.

'Sister?'

'Just drive, Corporal. Fast.'

Not even answers to a barrage of questions could quell Ivy's rising anxiety, 'When did you leave?' 'How much damage?' 'Were there others who died other than the colonel?'

On arrival at the clearing station gates, three soldiers stood in idle chatter. Inside, an eerie quiet greeted them. Lit by an almost full moon, a panorama of devastation lay before her. She closed her eyes. *She could be brave. She could be courageous.*

Ivy called for the corporal and the soldiers to follow as she raced from tent to tent. The medical tent, littered with strewn camp beds, lay abandoned. The two wooden buildings—one hosting the lieutenant-colonel's quarters—were splinters of wood burnt by cannon fire. She ran towards the men's quarters where collapsed tents fell on shattered wooden walkways.

A groan emanated from within Maurice's collapsed tent. But otherwise, it remained untouched.

'Lift the canvas!' she cried and crawled underneath. She could see a pair of legs trapped under a pole. 'Maurice!'

The men lifted the pole and raised the tent above them to drag in a stretcher. They carried Maurice across the compound and towards the waiting ambulance. Ivy walked next to him holding his hand.

Maurice's eyes blinked open when they lifted him inside. 'Am I in heaven?'

'No. You're injured,' she said and patted the sticky drying wound on his head with a cloth before kissing him. 'You stupid man.'

'You got my note then?'

'It went missing, but yes.'

His hand stroked her cheek.

'My legs hurt.'

'They're broken, and you have a nasty gash on your head. But we'll get it sorted.'

Ivy remained in the back with Maurice as they drove back to the base hospital. She dressed the wound on his head and splinted his legs.

'Does an apple a day keep the doctor away?' Maurice asked, his voice straining above the sound of the engine.

'Only if you aim it well enough,' she replied.

'I thought I was the funny one.' He gave a low groan.

She kissed him again. 'Tell better jokes, then.'

'Alright then. Sister—' He hummed and closed his eyes. 'A wasp stung me, have you got anything for it?'

'That is the least of your worries.' Ivy looked him over. 'Whereabouts is it?'

'I don't know, it could have flown miles away by now,' he said and chuckled.

'Your jokes are getting worse. Before you know it, you'll be back to your old self.' She squeezed his hand. 'Promise me, no more, you need to rest.'

'Promises are like babies: easy to make, hard to deliver.'

She responded with a quiet laugh and reached for another bandage. The sound of tearing fabric echoed and Ivy fingered the hole at her side. 'Oh.'

He struggled to raise his head up to look. 'What have you done?'

'It's nothing. I've only split my dress down the side.'

Maurice's chuckle turned into a hearty laugh.

'What are you laughing at?'

He ignored her question.

'Have you seen Captain Beaufort?'

'He's back at the hospital. Injured, but he'll recover.'

'Good, because he owes me twenty pounds.' He took her hand in his. 'You're very brave, your father and brother would be proud. *I'm proud.* I promise, no more joking if you give me another kiss.'

Having Maurice safe, and in her loving care, had fixed her heart.

'I love you, Captain Maurice Fletcher,' she said and laid her lips against his.

EPILOGUE

Portsmouth Docks, 1920

vy waved to her brothers and their families from the ships railings. Maurice stood beside her, nestling a small bundle of pudgy arms and legs in the crook of his arm.

'Are we doing the right thing, Maurice?' Ivy said, her heart pounding loud in her ears. They'd be travelling halfway around the world. Thousands of miles away from the green fields of England and Ireland, far from the fields of Flanders where they would harvest iron for years to come.

'What will our life be like?' she asked him.

He passed the gurgling infant to her and kissed her forehead. 'Where I grew up, they have pink Easter lilies.'

She kissed their daughter's hand and looked up to Maurice. 'Then we have hope.'

THE END

LE MALIN RENARD

By Ava January

CHAPTER 1

Snow floated in the air, in the whimsical, dancing way that only snow can.

Ariadne longed to stick her tongue out to catch it as she had done as a child, but settled for raising her face to the sky, eyes closed in bliss as she felt the snow fall on her face. In her mind, she was spinning in a circle, arms spread wide. She smiled, as the now familiar thrill stirred in her stomach in anticipation of a weekend that promised to be the best kind of fun.

The prickly feeling of eyes upon her brought her own open and her gaze met the warm brown regard of a—*good golly!*—very handsome fellow, watching her from the large window of the funicular station.

He sat with the impeccably straight posture of the well-bred, his expression unreadable. His brown hair was immaculately pomaded and smoothed to the side in the current fashion, impressively undamaged by the fedora which now sat in his lap. The tweed of his flawlessly cut suit hugged his broad shoulders in a way that spoke of expensive bespoke tailoring, and the fine grey stripe of the tweed picked up the strands of silver beginning to show at his temples.

Overall, a delicious specimen indeed.

Dipping her chin, she lifted a corner of her mouth, parting her lips just so. Instead of the expected smile in return, the object of her admiration simply raised a brow.

She blinked. *That wouldn't do.*

Fluttering her lashes, she turned the full force of her magnetic smile—no, this called for the knock-out smile.

Step one: run tongue along left corner of top lip, step two: cast eyes demurely to ground, step three: look back up to find him...

Staring at the timetable?

She ran her hand down the downy fur of her stole. He must have missed step one.

You're losing it.

She covered the mink stole's mouth and secured it more firmly upon its tail.

Ignoring the tingling at the back of her neck, she raised her chin haughtily and sashayed into the waiting room, adding an extra sway to her hips as she passed him.

She paused when she reached the corner of the room, pretending to be engrossed in the pamphlets lining the wall, while she took stock of the other patrons waiting.

The iron stove pinged as the logs within it burned slowly, the heat only just enough to take the chill from the air. Seven people sat on the bare, pine benches in the station, all wrapped up tightly against the unrelenting January weather. Their breaths were puffs of smoke in the cool air around them. Or perhaps, she thought with a small smirk, it was the soft scent of money wafting above their heads.

A slender woman sat at the back of the room, a silk scarf

tied around her hair and neck, her coat collar lifted against the cold. Despite the large dark glasses that partially obscured her face, it was clear by the glances and murmurs between a young debutante and her mother seated across from her, that she had been recognised as the famous ballerina, Valentina Komiskanokoff.

An elaborately elegant man sat on the bench along the wall opposite Ariadne, with a look of such disdain for his surroundings that she knew immediately he was a fellow French national. His valet sat dutifully beside him, a mountain of luggage almost completely masking him from view.

The door opened, bringing with it a burst of frigid air.

'Well, ain't this just jake.'

A large, well-dressed man stood in the doorway, surveying all waiting with the air of a man who is used to, and enjoys, all eyes upon him. His eyes darted from person to person, taking their measure, pausing ever so slightly on the debutante. He winked at her and she smiled coquettishly in return. With an efficient speed that spoke of experience, the young woman's mother whipped the book from her lap to shield her daughter from his view. Ariadne smiled as the girl peered around the spine of the book, eager to get another glimpse. Judging by his wolfish smile, it was clear it would take more than Sigmund Freud's words on the imagination to repel the attentions of one Mister Charles Parsons.

An American industrialist whose father had made his fortune in oil, he now surrounded himself with beauty. It was often said, although never to his face, that this was to hide the lack of it in his own heart.

Ariadne sat at the end of the closest bench and watched as he perused the room. His eyes moved from luggage to footwear before travelling slowly up the buttons of her coat. When their eyes finally met, Ariadne disdainfully raised an artistically manicured brow but he simply grinned back, unabashed, before making his way toward her with a studied nonchalance.

She bit back a smile.

More money than sense.

Her favourite type of tourist.

She watched Mr Broad-Shoulders tense as he followed the American's movements from the corner of his eye. He averted his face as Charles sat at the vacant end of her bench.

'Do you speak English?' the American asked loudly, as if the volume of his question would assist her in understanding it.

Ariadne turned toward him slightly, angling her body so the unblinking eyes of her mink stole could watch him carefully.

'Oui. Parlez vous Français?'

'Huh?'

'Yes, I speak English. Do you speak French?'

She adjusted her stole and his gaze caught on it a moment. He flinched slightly as he took in the beady glass eye and tiny, needle-like teeth.

Scoffing lightly as if she had said something ludicrous, he held his hand out towards her.

'Charles Parsons III. My pals call me Chuck.'

A mechanical screeching heralded the arrival of the funicular and saved her from further small talk. Which, she thought, keeping her eyes determinedly fixed upon his face, was almost certain to be unsatisfyingly small.

'Ladies and Gentleman, your carriage has arrived.' The voice of the sharply dressed conductor intoned from the doorway.

A general bustle began, as all waiting passengers made to gather their belongings with relief. She noticed Mr Sharp-Suit hovered at his seat a little, ensuring he was not standing before the ladies.

Chuck was first to the doorway.

Ariadne watched as Valentina feigned interest in her handbag and remained in her seat, pulling out a compact to retouch her make up.

The mother and daughter duo moved to the door and Ariadne followed, slowing as she passed where *he* stood, hat in hand. She stared at him until their eyes met and she tried again, one, two and...

Gotcha.

She blinked in surprise as a frisson passed between them. A burst of frigid air carried his scent, an intoxicating mix of musk, pine and pepper. His eyes were warm, melted chocolate and where his gaze rested on her lip, burnt as if scorched.

He inclined his head and it took her a moment to realise he was gesturing to the door.

She shook her head to clear it a little.

'Thank you,' she murmured throatily, moving from the room, grateful as the fresh air cooled her heated cheeks.

Running her hand along the stole, she covered its little glass eyes.

I don't want to hear a word from you.

The interior of the funicular was as spartan as the waiting room had been; worn, plain pine as far as the eye could see.

Ariadne chose the bench at the back of the carriage, the only one that would provide her with uninterrupted views of the guests as well as the snow-covered countryside as they ascended the cliff.

Chuck positioned himself across from the debutante and her mother, sharing another heated look with the young woman. He averted his face as her mother intercepted him fiercely.

Ariadne watched as her handsome fellow boarded. Unlike the peacocking of the French dandy and the American, he commanded attention without seeming to seek it out. The way he held himself, so stately and aloof, created an almost magnetic stillness around him.

The dandy flounced on, holding only his umbrella, leaving his valet to argue with the porter on the platform about the best way to pack his mountain of luggage on board.

As he passed, he raised a colluding eyebrow in her direction, which she responded to by staring vaguely over his shoulder. He stood for a moment, staring at her, before huffing away to settle himself mid-carriage.

A loud thump called everyone's attention to the back of the carriage, where the valet had dropped one of the myriad bags he was carrying.

His employer hissed at him from his seat as he struggled to right a hat box balancing precariously on top of one of the suitcases in his arms. The more he wrestled with the luggage, the less stable they all became.

The conductor sounded his whistle.

'Allez, allez!' the valet called in panic, gesturing with his head to the lone suitcase on the platform, arms still full. The conductor motioned back helplessly as the carriage began its ascent with the ear-piercing screech and squeal of metal on metal. The valet hastily dropped the bags and moved to the back of the carriage, screaming and gesturing frantically.

The broad-shouldered man placed his hat on the bench and strode to the back of the funicular.

'Throw it to me,' he commanded.

At the porter's blank look, he grasped the pole at the entrance of the carriage and leaned out a little, reaching his hand for the valise. The funicular continued its clattering up the hill, moving further away from the platform.

The debutante twisted in her seat to get a better view of the action and her mother made to rebuke her until she caught sight of him leaning from the carriage. An awed silence overtook the remaining passengers as they watched with collectively held breath.

'No way he can catch a suitcase like that!' Chuck exclaimed, half rising from his seat in excitement.

'Jetez-le moi,' the man called, as the carriage continued its ascent up the steep cliff.

The conductor lifted the suitcase to test its weight. He looked down at the suitcase in his hand and back to the carriage, before offering a gallic shrug and heaving it into the air.

The entire carriage held its breath as they tracked the arc of the case. For an agonising moment it seemed to hang suspended in air, at the peak of its apex. A gust of wind blew, catching the case and veering it just out of the man's reach.

He released his grip on the pole a little and leaned even further out. Ariadne's heart thumped in her throat as his foot slid on the bleached wood. After what seemed an age, his fingers grappled against the handle of the leather case, closing around it tightly as he swung himself back into the carriage. Leaning against the railing, he held the case against his chest, looking slightly dazed.

The entire carriage exhaled as one, before erupting into enthusiastic applause.

The noise jolted Ariadne back to reality and she realised her hand was clutching at her throat, her chest heaving as if it were she who had been leaning out into the abyss.

Her slightly stunned gaze met his wild one and the noise of the carriage fell away. All that existed was the sound of her own breath and his eyes. And lips.

Definitely those lips.

The valet ungraciously grabbed at the suitcase and the fleeting moment was gone and with it, the pressure in her chest.

Chuck moved forward to clap her man across the back in appreciation, as if he were a team member who had performed well. He brushed it off humbly, as if it were merely an insignificant act of kindness, as easy as returning a gentleman's hat after it had blown off in the wind.

Without appearing to put much thought into it, he sat at the end of Ariadne's bench keeping his eyes trained on the floor at his feet. She tickled her fingers through the silky fur of her stole to still her anxious hands.

As the tension that had squeezed them so tightly finally released its hold, everyone started to talk at once, emboldened by the excitement they had just witnessed.

'Y'all coming up for the exhibition?' Chuck addressed no one in particular, or more likely, addressed them all.

An abrupt silence ensued.

Valentina looked out the window and adjusted her dark glasses. The debutante and her mother cast their eyes to their laps. The dandy was suddenly engrossed in a whispered conversation with his valet.

Several weeks ago, fifteen cream linen invitations had fallen and flown through letterboxes around the world. The names of the passengers in the funicular had been hand-written upon the front of seven of them. An art auction like no other was to be held at The Hotel Lilâ, currently considered the most luxurious hotel in Europe. Accessible only by one funicular that clattered up and down the steep cliff-side, the former Chateau was now considered to be the most exclusive and remote hotel France had to offer.

The invitations had expressly demanded discretion and no return name or address had been offered. A standard post office address in London had been provided for RSVPs.

'You like art?' Chuck said to the debutante, who responded with a giggle. Her mother tapped her on the leg with her book firmly, before answering on her behalf.

'My daughter is studying art history at Oxford university. My husband, that is, her father, is expected here tomorrow. We are most interested in the Van Dyck.'

The American licked the corner of his mouth.

'Y'all heard the rumour there will be a Faberge egg as well?'

For the second time in mere minutes, the carriage seemed

to collectively hold its breath. The dandy and the valet ceased their whispering in French, cautious eyes darting to where Chuck loomed over the ladies.

In the weeks that followed the receipt of the invite, padded envelopes had arrived bi-weekly, with coloured illustrations of rare artwork. Although no note was included, it was assumed they were the works that would be auctioned. The final envelope had included a picture of Princess Alix of Hesse with a distinctive Faberge egg visible behind her left shoulder.

'Of course,' the mother said. 'We heard a *rumour* one would be on display.'

'The Rosebud.'

All heads swivelled to the Russian ballerina.

She removed her sunglasses and turned to the rest of the carriage, her eyes red rimmed in her pale face.

'The Rosebud is to be auctioned. It is said that Princess Alix missed her home of Rosenhöhe and its famous rose gardens so much that Nicholas II had the egg made for their first Easter together. There is a surprise inside - a symbol of his undying devotion, and the egg itself symbolises her rebirth as a Russian aristocrat.'

Chuck stared at her long and hard and seemed to be on the verge of saying something when the French dandy spoke.

'The surprise inside is a ruby necklace with the single largest ruby ever found.'

'Not to mention there may be a Cézanne on offer,' the debutante piped up, seemingly eager to change the subject.

An earnest conversation began about the merits of romantic versus impressionist art. Ariadne turned to see her man was watching the characters in the carriage with a simmering quietness.

'Forgive me if I say you don't look like an art collector,' she said lightly.

One corner of his mouth lifted ever so slightly.

'No? What *does* an art collector look like?'

She gestured with her eyes to the large American, now occupying a bench seat in its entirety. Legs spread; arms outstretched along the backrest, with a wide grin designed to show off his large, vividly white teeth.

She smirked and he tilted his head to the side in response.

When his eyes met hers again, she raised an eyebrow toward the dandy, his lime green bow tie the perfect colour match to the ribbon on his hat.

He coughed into his hand in response.

'Quite. Well in that case, I am happy not to look like an art collector. Are you?'

'Oh no. I am a lover of beauty, but a collector? Non. The very things we find beautiful cease to be so once we own them and can gaze upon them every day.'

He raised an eyebrow.

'It is human nature is it not?' she asked mildly.

'Not always,' he said quietly, 'sometimes the beauty is in the knowing.'

Something pulled at her chest and she averted her gaze out the window. The funicular moved over the crest of the cliff and the chateau finally came into view. A vast grey building perched on the edge of the cliff, it appeared to be hewn directly from the cliff-side itself, the granite blending in effortlessly with the grey rock behind. Snow covered the roof and tops of trees, giving the impression of a cake generously sprinkled with sugar.

She let out a small sigh of appreciation.

Turning to make a comment about its magnificence, she found her seat mate studying her with an intensity that took her breath away.

Their eyes locked for a brief moment before wordlessly, he turned his gaze back toward the castle.

A bell rang and the screeching noise that indicated they were coming to stop sounded again. The funicular pulled into a tunnel that housed the disembarking point for guests of the hotel, where the white-coated staff milled about efficiently. One stood at the doorway to assist the passengers in alighting and Ariadne held his soft cottoned hand as she hopped nimbly from the carriage.

The frigid breeze whistled in her ears. The wind was stronger up here, more combative in its approach. No longer a gentle caress, it pushed and battered, forced you to do its bidding.

A tall gentleman dressed in the all-white ensemble of the hotel uniform tucked her under an umbrella and ushered her inside.

If she had been made breathless by the beauty of the exterior of the Chateau then she was stunned by the inside. Lush red carpet, gold trims, and expansive candelabras hung from the ceiling. A fire roared in the double fireplace in the centre of the lobby, creating a welcoming warmth that belied the weather outside. A large stone staircase curved back upon itself, its wrought iron railings as intricate and delicate as dew covered cobwebs. No expense had been spared in the restoration of the Chateau. It was luxurious, glamourous and most importantly, warm.

'Your invitation madam?'

The porter held out his hand and she unlatched her bag to retrieve it from where it had been carefully tucked into the folds of a book. She watched as he vigilantly inspected her ticket, polite but unwilling to assume its veracity. He performed his checks and finally handed it back to her, smiling generously as he gestured to the stairwell.

She stepped quietly behind him as he carried her luggage, only half listening to his welcoming speech as the magic of the chateau enchanted her. She ran her hand along the railing gently—how many other people had done exactly that? How many love stories and betrayals had played out between these dense, unforgiving walls?

They made their way down the carpeted hallway, passing door after indistinguishable door until they reached the end of the hall where two lone doors faced each other.

She watched as the porter carefully extracted a master key from a crowded ring on his belt. Unlocking the door and holding it wide with one arm, he ushered her past him with the other.

Her breath caught in delight as the vista of the snow-covered alps appeared.

'C'est magnifique, oui?'

'Oui,' she replied simply. It was the most incredible view she had seen of her beloved country and for a fleeting moment, she almost, *almost* wished this weekend was something other than what it was.

The porter stowed her luggage, clicking his heels to gain her attention when he had finished.

'A pre-lunch aperitif will be served in thirty minutes. Please you come to the lobby bar at your convenience.'

He gave an elaborate bow and backed out of the room, bent double, his eyes never leaving hers until the door fully closed. She carefully worked Minky's jaw to remove his soft tail from his mouth, patting his dry little button nose as she did so.

He likes you.

Maybe, but he wasn't the one she was interested in.

She stretched Minky out on the bed, ensuring his glass eyes were pointed to the beautiful vista out the window. She unsnapped her suitcase, unfolding the carefully packed peach beaded dress she would be wearing for luncheon. Unbuttoning her travelling coat, she slid it from her shoulders, letting it pool on the floor. Her dress was next and she shimmied out of it before flicking it to the corner of the room with her toe, smiling as it landed on the fringed lamp upon the desk.

She primped and preened with a swift expertise that spoke of many nights spent in hotel rooms and quick changes, and found herself ready to indulge in an aperitif only twenty minutes after the allotted time.

On time by anyone's standards.

Trailing her hand lightly along the balustrade of the stairs, she studied her surroundings. Due to the age of the chateau, the stairwell was enclosed and dimly lit and should one wish to remain unseen they would be easily able to do so by keeping close to the wall.

The stairs deposited its sojourners into the reception lobby, an octagon with one long hallway opposite the desk. She assumed it led to the kitchen, the servant's quarters and offered toilette options for the guests enjoying dinner downstairs.

A set of double doors led to the vast dining area, which

encompassed the entire corner of the chateau. Surrounded by a terraced balcony, the room made the most of the magnificent views over the alps. Ariadne smiled as she saw the lone figure of her broad-shouldered man standing on the other side of the glass, smoking a cigarette, his face turned towards the mountainside. A magnetic force urged her through the dining room, her feet almost skipping across the thick carpet as she moved from the warmth of the Chateau out into the flurry of snow. They stood silently, shoulder to shoulder for a moment before she spoke.

'We didn't get the opportunity to introduce ourselves earlier.'

He glanced down at her outstretched hand and for one exciting moment she wondered if he was going to accept it. When he did finally wrap his gloved hand around hers, a rush of electricity moved between them, from his hand to hers, moving up her body before it burst out on a smile.

'Evander Jones. And you are?'

'Ariadne Aries.' She allowed her gaze to rest on him a moment, drinking in the hint of stubble on his jaw, the depth of his eyes, the luscious fullness of his lips. 'What a pleasure it is to meet you.'

The door rattled loudly behind them, interrupting whatever Evander had been about to say in reply.

They watched in quiet amusement as Chuck jiggled at the door handle, fruitlessly pulling the door toward him. He pulled at the matching door beside it, jiggling furiously before Evander leaned forward to pull the French door toward them.

'Push,' Evander said lightly.

'Huh?' Chuck responded, in the plain-speaking way men like him preferred. 'You know, someone oughta tell the French about the doors we have back home. They spin around, always spinning, and you just step in, you know?'

Evander and Ariadne's eyes caught as Chuck's monologue about doors continued and she bit lightly on the end of her cigarette holder to stop from laughing.

Evander cupped his hand around the end of her cigarette as he lit it for her. She held his gaze as she blew a long plume of smoke into the air around them.

'So, you two in the market for some art?' Chuck asked.

Ariadne took in the set of his jaw, the hardness of his eyes and the meaty hand that fisted against his leg.

She raised a brow.

'Perhaps. But only if something takes my interest.' She shifted her gaze to Evander with her final word.

Chuck glanced at Evander and she watched with amusement as they sized each other up silently.

'No,' Evander said plainly, taking a deep draw on his cigarette.

Chuck stared at him, a deep red flush moving up his neck and Ariadne had a sense that for all his foolish blustering, he might well be a formidable opponent.

'Oh yeah? Well pal, it is an invite only event for the most important people in the art world.'

Evander made a show of looking around the vacant patio where piles of snow were building on the abandoned tables, before raising his brows mockingly.

Chuck smiled instead of taking offence.

Tapping his nose, he winked at Evander. 'Ok, swell, I gotcha now.' He clapped him on the back. 'Your secret's safe with me, pal.'

Evander looked down at where Chuck's hand sat on his shoulder like a hock of ham, before flicking his eyes up to meet his.

Before the words that were forming on his perfect lips made the trouble they had been about to, a bell sounded somewhere on the grounds, heralding the beginning of lunch.

'My favourite sound,' Ariadne said lightly, offering her arm to Evander. 'Shall we?'

He ground his cigarette beneath the heel of his boot and took her arm. Chuck opened the door, correctly this time, ushering them into the blessed warmth.

'Who exactly does he believe you to be?' Ariadne

murmured from the corner of her mouth.

'Absolutely no idea,' Evander returned with a sound that was almost, *almost* a laugh.

The lounge was already simmering with guests, the white uniformed waiters moving expertly between them, providing delicate gold gilded glasses filled with creamy bubbles.

The newly arrived guests were being eyed warily by a round, red faced couple, muttering to each in German, who had arrived at the hotel the day before. The art studying debutante and her mother arrived and, having changed for lunch, appeared much less travel wearied. The young woman looked up as they entered the room, blushing prettily when she spied Chuck. Her mother offered a stiff smile in Ariadne's direction, entirely uncertain as to her suitability. She was clearly torn - Ariadne obviously important enough to warrant an invite to this event but far too glamorous for decorum's sake.

Was anyone so obsessed with their reputation as the English, Ariadne thought with disdain.

She accepted a glass from the offered tray and noticed with amusement how the French dandy stood apart from the group, affecting an avid inspection of the artwork on the walls, while ensuring he remained within earshot of the group's conversation. His valet stood beside him, staring moodily out the window at the rising snowstorm.

Chuck held his glass aloft.

'Cheers to an exciting weekend.'

He gestured with his eyebrows and a tilt of the head toward the debutante.

'What's your name cutie pie? I didn't catch it earlier.'

Her mother winced at his gaucheness, her lips pursed tightly.

'This is Miss Francine Smythe and I am Mrs Archibald Smythe.' Again she spoke for her daughter.

Was it her imagination or had there been an ever-so-slight emphasis on the unmarried title of her daughter?

'Oh, do please call me Fanny,' the young woman offered breathlessly as Chuck lunged at a passing waiter.

'I say old chap, can we catch sight of the egg?'

The waiter smiled politely.

'Pardon. The exhibition does not start until tomorrow evening, sir.'

'Is it here though?' Chuck pressed.

The waiter moved on with little more than a tilt of his head. Chuck's narrowed gaze followed him on his route.

'Oh, I do hope it will be on display,' Fanny said earnestly. 'One never knows if these rumours are simply thrown out there with the express purpose of getting our hopes up.'

Chuck glanced at Evander briefly, where he stood a little apart from the group.

'I have it on good authority it will not only be on display, Miss Smythe, but it will be available for purchase.'

At the excited gasps his proclamation received, Chuck continued, 'I am not a man whose time you would wish to waste with idle rumours.'

His self-important words had the desired effect on Fanny and she fluttered her lashes at him vigorously. Even the disapproving mother seemed to be thawing.

Funny how money had such a warming effect on people of a certain ilk.

Talk turned to the chateau and the breathtaking views they had all discovered from their bedroom windows, before circling around to speculation of who the other guests arriving for tomorrow's exhibition would be.

'I heard Princess Antoinette of Monaco will be in attendance—'

'—Daniel Guggenheim.'

'—and the Count of Kyburg too.'

With each name, Chuck became more and more morose.

'Do you think they want artwork?' he asked transparently. 'Most people are here for the art, aren't they?'

The Frenchman decided to add his kindle to the fire.

'Surely *everyone* is interested in The Rosebud egg, no?' His valet's head shot around to glare fiercely at him.

'In fact,' he went on, 'there is so much interest that the famous thief, we call Le Malin Renard, is rumoured to be attending.' He looked squarely at Evander. 'Isn't that right, Inspector?'

All eyes swung to where Evander stood, watching them all silently.

Evander narrowed his eyes. 'You tell me, Monsieur...?'

'De Lisle,' the Frenchman said and Evander nodded in return.

'De Lisle, of the famed De Lisle house, sent into poverty by a reckless, drunkard. Your father, I presume?'

At De Lisle's horrified look, Evander warned coldly, 'Everyone has secrets.'

Ariadne smiled into her champagne glass at his response. *Didn't they indeed.*

All at once, a burst of wind rattled the glass in its panes, a door slammed and the Hotel Manager, Jean-Luc, appeared in the doorway, breathing heavily.

'I am afraid...' Jean-Luc paused and took a moment to smooth his hair and adjust his waistcoat, aware that his voice had betrayed his unease.

'I am afraid there has been an incident. A snowdrift has fallen into the funicular station. The snow has picked up, as you can see.' At his words, all eyes swung to the window where indeed, snow now swirled around the panes ominously.

'The funicular cannot be moved. The snow has trapped it.'

The announcement was met with silence and his mouth

worked as he realised he was going to need to be clearer.

'The funicular is out of order, however, it will be of no consequence to you. We have a team of men working to rectify it now.'

There was a collective gasp as the meaning of his words sunk in.

'We're stranded?'

'No one else can get up the mountain?'

'Is the egg already on site?'

Oh Chuck.

Jean-Luc held up his hands to stall the flow of questions.

'This is a common occurrence this time of year, one we are well versed in managing. The team of men are working to clear the snow but I am afraid –' he pressed his fist to his lips. '–if the winds keep up then the funicular will not be safe for use.'

'How will the other guests get to the hotel?' Mrs Smythe asked.

'There is no other route to the hotel madam. We are accessible only by the funicular. However, it should not take more than a day,' he said into the silence that met his statement.

'But my husband...' Mrs Smythe faltered. 'He is to join us tomorrow for the auction.'

'Madam, I can assure you we will be doing everything we can to ensure the funicular is open in time for the arrival of the other guests tomorrow. The auction will still proceed as planned.'

The manager bowed toward Mrs Smythe, his eyes trained hard on the floor as he backed out of the room as quickly as he could.

Ten pairs of eyes were suddenly captivated by their glasses, the wall, their shoes and the silence shimmered with a disquiet that would have set the bravest teeth on edge.

CHAPTER 5

he evening bell rang and Ariadne's heart thumped
in her chest.

Moving quickly to the door, she pressed her ear pressed
gently against the wood, listening intently for the noise of
movement in the hallway.

The lunch had passed without further discord, as if
everyone was on their best behaviour. They had eaten,
laughed and listened but, ever so carefully, no further
mention of the art auction was made.

Finally, the sound she had been listening for—the click
and thump of the door directly opposite hers and the strong,
steady footfalls of its occupant as he made his way down to
the lobby.

She counted quietly in her head, ignoring the baleful stare
of the mink stole, where it lay discarded upon the bed. He
did so hate missing out on the action, but there was little call
for a stole in the well heated hotel.

With one last glance in the mirror, she stepped out into
the quiet hallway. The echoes and excited murmurings of the
guests rose up to meet her as she descended the stairs.

Trailing her hand lightly along the freshly oiled balustrade, she measured her steps. The chatter stilled as she came into view, the glass beads on the fringe of her dress swinging and reflecting the light as she descended.

Chuck let out a low whistle and she smiled coyly. Her eyes locked with Evander's and that same smile quickly transformed to a genuine one. His expression didn't change but, she noticed, his eyes never left hers.

When she reached the bottom step, Jean-Luc was at her right elbow instantly, offering a glass of champagne, which she gracefully accepted. She stood a moment, aware that the staircase behind framed her perfectly. The red carpet runner created a warm glow on the creamy silk that hugged her body in a way that would have been considered illegal a mere decade ago.

'Inspector,' she murmured in greeting.

'You look...'

At his pause, she placed a delicate hand on her hip.

He swallowed.

'Incredible doesn't quite cut it,' he said finally.

She ran her gaze down his immaculately pressed tuxedo.

'You, also.'

They stared at each other steadily a moment before he broke the spell by raising his eyebrows.

'May I?' he asked, as he presented her with his elbow, asking her if he could accompany her into the ballroom.

'You may.'

The heat of his arm pressed against hers made her shiver slightly and she rested her hand against his arm, where their arms met.

The ruddy German couple were already seated at a table in the restaurant, the woman with a small, fluffy dog tucked under her arm. They smiled welcomely as they walked in, gesturing in invitation to the long table they sat at. At their request, the waiters had joined the tables together to allow them all to sit and eat as a group.

The night moved in the timeless way it does when there is nowhere else to go. Bonded by the lack of outsiders and free flowing wine, the mood in the dining room was convivial and strangely celebratory, despite the murderous weather outside.

Surprisingly, Chuck was a fabulous dinner party guest, regaling them with stories of the wacky, wealthy members of American society. He name-dropped again and again, much to the delight of Fanny. Even her mother seemed to enjoy his anecdote about an evening at the theatre punctuated by a showdown between Caroline Astor Wilson and her husband's mistress.

Where Ariadne sat across from Chuck, on Evander's right, with Valentina on his left, conversation was much more subdued.

Valentina spent the meal pushing food around her plate, looking for places to hide it. Without the dark glasses, Ariadne saw how pale and unhappy the woman appeared.

Ariadne watched as Fanny laughed at something Chuck said, throwing her head back, before leaning toward him earnestly, resting her hand lightly on his shoulder.

Valentina was caught in discussion with the German man, her face a picture of disdain as he earnestly gesticulated with his fork. His wife fed her little dog on her lap while she discussed her neighbours in Berlin with Mrs Smythe. They must have been impressive neighbours, as Mrs Smythe kept her eyes studiously averted while the dog licked cream from its owner's fingers.

Evander was polite and attentive but she sensed his distraction. He watched the other guests with a razor-sharp gaze and there was something about the way he held himself, as if ready to spring into action at any moment, that had her captivated.

Although his face remained impassive, she noticed how often his gaze swung to the Frenchman, where he sat sullenly beside his valet.

Ariadne longed to run her hand along the sharp crease of Evander's trouser leg. It wasn't until dessert was served that he finally allowed his spine to touch the back of the chair.

Chuck leaned across the table. 'So, Inspector.' His voice was a little too loud, his face flushed. 'Tell me. Why are you here?'

All eyes were on Evander but it was De Lisle who spoke.

'Our inspector is here hunting the one we call *Le Malin Renard*. Is that not correct?'

Evander levelled the man with a cool stare but nodded.

'That is true. I work for the International Criminal Police Commission and we are on the trail of a thief who calls himself The Clever Fox.'

'He is very famous in France,' the Frenchman said, with a satisfied smirk. 'The press love to report how he eludes your clutches time and time again.'

Ariadne's eyes were drawn to a muscle pulsing at Evander's neck.

'Is that so?'

'It is. They say that you are always one step behind. He walks out the back door of the Louvre while you walk in the front,' De Lisle said with a mocking laugh. 'He has stolen some of the world's most expensive artefacts.'

Chuck swirled the wine in his glass before holding it up to the light, peering at it through one eye.

'You think *he* is here for the egg?

Evander smiled tightly.

'All I can tell you is that if he is, then I am here for him.'

Silence swirled around them for a beat, then two. The

ruddy faced German man cleared his throat and asked Chuck a question about the stock market, and table talk turned to other matters. Awareness prickled along her skin and Ariadne looked up to find Evander studying her. She placed her hand under her face to frame it and offered him her sweetest smile.

'Do I pass the test?'

'What test?' he asked and she cocked her head at him, narrowing her eyes.

'I see you analysing everyone here. On the lookout for Renard.' She lowered her voice and widened her eyes as she said the name. 'You don't really think he is here, do you? Why don't you just relax? There is no one here but us.'

He took a deep, weary breath before closing his eyes and leaning his head back against the chair. Suddenly she saw that he didn't relax, he never took a day or night off. He was consumed by finding this Renard and it was eating him alive.

'Why do you care so much?' Ariadne asked quietly. 'Why does it matter to you if rich people have things taken from them? Things they can easily afford to replace?'

He stared at her silently and she was again struck by the colour of his eyes.

Finally, he sighed, rubbing his hand down his face as he looked to the ceiling, as if appealing for answers.

'Why? I ask myself that. Why do I care so much. What is it about him?'

He lowered his head and their eyes met.

'Since the war, I need to believe that for every bad man out there, there is an equally good one. One just as willing to do whatever it takes. He is the other side of my coin. And yes, he has got the better of me. He toys with me, sometimes leaving items from his last theft at the next one for me to find, so I know it is him. He wants me to find him. It has to be me.'

He looked at her, the light making his eyes appear even darker, even deeper than they had during the day.

'Have you ever seen him?' she asked.

'No one has ever seen him. He's ten-foot-tall, he's a spectre, a demon. He's Robin Hood stealing from the rich to give to the poor. A genius, a mastermind.'

She raised her eyebrows in delight.

'He sounds incredible. Handsome too, no?'

His mouth moved in the tantalising way it did when he was working to hold back a smile.

'Not as handsome as you, I bet.'

He narrowed his eyes at her and she widened her own in return.

She ran her finger slowly along the edge of her champagne flute, watching as his eyes followed its path. Raising it to her lips, she paused, suddenly unnerved to find that this well-worn path of seduction was having an effect on her too.

'Perhaps it is because he is smarter than you, no?'

She laughed at his expression and clutched at her chest.

'Oh la la, the look that kills.'

'He is not smarter than me,' he returned firmly.

'Oh? He outwits you again and again. It sounds to me like he is a *little* smarter than you.'

He levelled her with another look and she rested her hand lightly on his leg, leaning toward him. His gaze rested on her hand as she whispered throatily in his ear.

'At least we know it couldn't possibly be the American.'

He turned his head away, raising his fist to his mouth and she was certain she had made him smile but when he looked back at her, his expression was as neutral as ever.

'Perhaps without Renard, I have nothing.'

Ariadne ran her finger lightly along his hand where it sat on the table between them before turning it palm up.

Running her hand over his, she thrilled at the feeling of his flesh beneath her own.

'Shall I tell your fortune?' she murmured.

His hand flexed under hers but to her delight, he didn't pull it away.

'Can you?'

'Oui.' She traced her thumb along his ring finger.

'Unmarried.'

He raised his eyebrows mockingly.

'No ring. What a deduction.'

She stroked the fleshy mound of his thumb.

'You are a man most restrained, but of enormous sensuality.' Turning his hand over, she wound her fingers through his. She traced the outline of an old scar on his knuckle and longed to press it to her lips. His eyes were closed, his lips parted slightly and when he felt her eyes upon him they snapped open.

Suddenly, she was caught. The hunter was now the hunted and her little game no longer felt as safe as it had a moment ago. His eyes burned with a fire that threatened to consume her but instead of being wary of the flame, she was drawn to it.

No matter that she knew she was the worst kind of matchwood. The kind that burned everything around it, as well as consuming itself.

'This Renard,' she said, 'he will destroy you. He will take your goodness, your spirit and he will consume it.'

Her chest squeezed, as a heaviness weighed upon her, a weight she had no desire to explore.

'Do you let anyone in, Inspector?' she asked and the rasp of her voice was no longer just for effect. 'Do not let a petty criminal take your life.'

'I know him,' he said roughly. 'I just feel... I might be the only one who truly understands how his mind works, so I am the only one who can stop him.'

'Well, isn't that all we really want? To be truly seen and understood by another? Isn't that all we are all seeking?'

He suddenly flipped his hand and grasped hers, bringing her fingers to his lips, so quickly, so fleetingly, that she stared at it a moment where it again rested on the table, wondering if she had imagined it.

'That is my fortune? That I am destined to find my soul-mate but it is a thieving scoundrel?'

She smiled.

'Just so. At least it is the best one the world has ever seen, no?'

The evening wore on and the dinner service was cleared in preparation for the jazz singer, setting up at the front of the room.

'If you will excuse me,' Ariadne stood from the table and Evander and Chuck half rose from their chairs.

The Frenchman remained seated.

Fanny quickly folded her napkin and placed it on the table beside her plate, signalling with her eyebrows to Ariadne she wished to join her.

'Myself also, gentlemen.'

Ariadne offered the young girl her arm and they walked quickly from the room, Fanny adjusting her gait to match Ariadne's, ignoring the censorious stare of her mother.

Ariadne was pleasantly surprised to find the girl was able to hold her tongue until the double doors leading to the reception foyer were closed behind them.

'Oh, Miss Aries,' she gasped, fanning her face as she leaned dramatically against the wall. 'Whatever is a girl to do? Charles is just the most handsome thing, isn't he? Oh, do say you aren't planning on warning me off him.'

With that, she straightened her hands, clasping them together at her waist.

'Warn you off New York's wealthiest bachelor? Why ever would I do that?' Ariadne questioned lightly, continuing towards the ladies' room in the narrow, dimly lit hallway.

They entered together, the younger girl still babbling about Chuck, seemingly grateful to have someone to share a confidence with. It was doubtful her mother was interested in dissecting Chuck's tidbits such as the utter modernness of his tie and charming colour of his eyes.

Still, there was only one set of eyes Ariadne was interested in.

'Fanny,' she said firmly once they were in the ladies' room. 'There is something you should know about Chuck.'

She pulled the younger lady around to face her, holding her delicate hands in her own.

'He is here to buy the Faberge egg as an engagement gift for Isabella Vanderbilt.'

Fanny's face fell.

'But—'

'He is toying with you, my dear. He is charming you in the hopes that he can dissuade you from bidding for the egg.'

'But that is ridiculous!' Fanny burst out, her cheeks burning brightly. 'I'm not...'

She stopped herself before looking sadly at Ariadne.

'We aren't in the market for a Faberge egg. Our father isn't on his way. He has left my mother for another woman and she was...that is *we* were hoping...' the girl faltered and stopped.

'You were hoping to meet a rich man before the scandal became known?'

At Fanny's small nod, Ariadne asked, 'How did you receive an invite?'

'My father is a well-known art professor and prolific

collector and I am currently making a name for myself at Oxford. I was one of the only students to get a first in Art History last year.'

She stood taller, her pride in herself not completely demolished.

Yet.

It wouldn't be long before the scandal hit the important parts of society and she found herself cut socially.

'But without him...'

Ariadne patted her hand, where it was still clasped in her own.

'I understand. A woman must do what she can to protect herself. But Chuck is not your salvation. You would be better off returning to Oxford and finding a man who shares your passion for art history.'

The door swung open and the ladies turned in surprise to find Valentina leaning against the doorjamb.

She perused them coolly.

'Goodbye Ladies.'

Fanny's eyebrows shot to her hairline.

'I beg your pardon?'

Ariadne watched as Valentina struggled to stand upright, resting all her weight on one foot only.

'You go. Valentina does not share her bathroom,' Valentina said archly.

Fanny shot Ariadne a look and she smiled politely.

'We were finished. Come, Fanny.'

She held her arm out for Fanny to take but they were unable to move through the doorway while Valentina stood in it. Ariadne watched as she fought to keep the look of pain from her face as she stepped into the bathroom around the ladies.

'If her privacy is so important why doesn't she use the bathroom in her own bedroom,' Fanny sniffed, as they exited the room. Ariadne glanced up as De Lisle's valet strode past them purposefully.

'She's injured,' she said, turning back to Fanny only when the valet had left her sight.

Fanny gasped in shock.

'But she's the most famous ballerina in the world!' she exclaimed.

'She can barely stand. She is unable to make the stairs more than once a night.'

Fanny stared at the closed bathroom door, her eyes narrowed.

A moment passed as she seemed to consider something.

'Really,' was all she offered.

Smiling brightly, she turned to Ariadne and offered her arm as they walked back together into the dining room.

CHAPTER 7

The band had started and were playing a familiar and widely popular chanson. The guests that hadn't gotten up to dance had turned their chairs to watch the performance.

Ariadne noted Evander's tapping foot under his chair.

'Will you ask me to dance, inspector?'

Evander didn't speak, instead simply offered her his hand, and she pulled him gently to his feet.

They walked to the dance floor hand in hand, pausing at the edge of the highly polished parquetry floor that signalled the dancing space. He didn't release her hand as the final notes of the current song played, nor in the quiet moments after. When the band started the first few notes of a ballad, he led her out on to the floor, carefully encircling her in his arms.

She rested her head against his shoulder, it was impossible not to notice that it fitted perfectly. As if the entire reason for his broad shoulders was to make space for her to rest her weary head. As if his shoulders were a pillar of strength she could lay her woes upon, without them ever crumbling or buckling under their weight.

She knew there would only be this night for them. Once the funicular opened and the real world descended upon them, tonight would be nothing but a memory to keep her warm. There was no possibility for them.

She breathed in his scent, cherishing every note of it before closing her eyes and allowing her body to move in time with his, led totally by his movements only. He moved with an ease that was surprising. Like he was finally free to release all the emotions he held so tightly during the day. The consummate gentleman, he held her gently, his strong arms barely touching her but where they did, her skin burned, longing for his touch. Her hand arched and flexed on his shoulder, longing to run down his arm, to feel the muscle underneath his woollen jacket.

His breath in her ear was as even as the heartbeat she could feel against her cheek. What would this man look like untrussed, unbidden, unleashed? Would he tether his desire or would he let go and release the passionate man that burned beneath the surface of his public face. The good man, the righteous man. Did he feel her zinging under his skin whenever she was near, the way she did with him?

His breath stilled and she looked up, her gaze clashing with his.

His eyes burned with an elemental fire. She bit her lip in an empty parody of her practised move, for it was her who was now caught. She was unable to pull her gaze away from his as he leaned tantalisingly close to her mouth. His gaze dropped to her lips as he moved closer, as if a magnetic force propelled him. She closed her eyes in anticipation of his mouth against hers but the sweet release never came. She snapped her eyes open to find him staring at her. He lightly brushed a stray hair from her face, his touch feather light. She fought the urge to press her face against his hand.

She smiled at him languidly.

'Would you care to walk me to my room?'

His gaze was fathomless, her unsmiling man. He appeared to be considering something and when he finally spoke, his voice was ragged with desire.

'I won't be able to stop at your door.'

She held his gaze boldly.

'I was hoping you wouldn't.'

Although the music played on, he halted mid-step, causing her body to crush against his and a thrill went through her as she felt the hard planes of his body against hers.

He dropped his arm from their dancing pose but did not release her hand, instead tucking it into the crook of his arm before striding purposefully from the room.

They burst through the double doors of the restaurant with an eagerness that awoke the hotel receptionist where he had been slumbering at the desk.

At his alarmed look she fought back a laugh and Evander saluted him jauntily.

'Keep up the good work, old chap.'

Her laughter bubbled and Evander turned to look at her. The world seemed to tilt on its very axis. Angels descended from the ceiling, their shiny trumpets polished and at the ready. Cupid lifted his bow and took aim. Fireworks exploded around them and finally—*finally!*—he smiled at her.

Her heart stopped with an alarming pain as Cupid's bow hit its mark and she clutched at her chest.

He stilled, his face concerned. She lifted her hand to his face.

'You smiled,' she said in wonderment. 'Oh, good lord. What a smile.'

To her delight he did it again and her heart kick-started roughly.

'Play your cards right and there's more where that came from.'

Joy burst free on a laugh and she raced up the stairs lightly.

'Don't leave me waiting,' she called over her shoulder.

He chased her, laughing all the way up, the sound of it bringing a lightness to her heart she had long ago forgotten she was capable of.

Finally, they reach the top of the staircase and there was a moment of stillness between them.

'Your room or mine?' he asked, gesturing first to her door and then to his, directly across the hallway.

She ran her hand up the lapels of his evening jacket, thrilling at the feel of his muscular chest beneath her fingers. Pressing herself against him she lowered her eyes demurely.

'I wasn't planning... that is... I would be embarrassed. By the mess.'

'My room it is then,' he growled.

Suddenly his hands were in her hair and his lips against hers and it was unlike any thrill she had ever chased, any high she had ever reached. He lifted her into his arms, his lips never breaking from hers. Carrying her to his door, he pressed her body against the hard wood while he fumbled for his key. A moan, a sound deep in his chest, a sound of such wanting, of such need, broke free and unleashed something in her. It no longer mattered that they were in the hallway of a hotel, all she knew was that she needed his hands on her.

Finally, the door opened, he pulled away from her allowing her to enter the room first, his hand never leaving hers. Her eyes roamed the room, cataloguing the perfect precision of his razor and comb on the basin in the corner of the room and her heart squeezed so tightly in her chest she feared she would not be able to take her next breath. The longing she felt for him raised to a crescendo as he ran his hands down her arms, lowering his lips to her neck.

'If you have changed your mind you are free to leave at any time.'

She turned to him, winding her arms around his neck, before lifting her face to his. The thrill of being so close to him ran through her like electricity.

'Oh no. I have plans for you.'

CHAPTER 8

$\mathcal{E}$vander woke with the sense of having just left the most delicious dream. He almost moaned aloud as the memories of last night came flooding back and his muscles ached pleasurably as he rolled onto his back.

He slid his hand along the cool sheet towards her pillow, hoping to make contact with her warm, soft body, only to find nothing but cool linen.

He cracked an eyelid, surprised to find her side of the bed bare, with nothing to show for it but wrinkles where her head had lain. He pulled her pillow to him, pressing his face against it, luxuriating in her scent.

What a woman. She was joy personified.

A rumble of excited voices in the hallway interrupted his musings on how they would spend the rest of their day, before a quick rap on his door had him sitting to attention in bed. His feet were on the ground, the sheet wrapped around his waist as he moved toward the door.

'Sir?'

His heart dropped, not Ariadne then.

The rap sounded again, more urgent this time.

'Sir, are you in there?'

He pulled the door open to find the usually immaculately dressed Jean-Luc standing before him, his shirt buttoned incorrectly, his face ashen.

Evander watched as the manager's Adam's apple worked up and down and his stomach clenched. He balled his hand into a fist at his leg.

'It's the egg sir, I'm afraid. It's missing.' The manager confirmed and a burst of hot rage surged through Evander. A screech sounded from the hallway and Jean-Luc winced.

'It appears a diamond brooch has also been stolen from Miss Komiskanokoff's room.'

A flurry of angry Russian was broadcast down the hallway and Jean-Luc looked around nervously.

'It was given to her by her lover who has broken her heart by returning to his wife and she would very much like it back.'

'When were they stolen?'

'I am afraid we do not know. Sometime in the early hours of this morning.'

'Where? How? Goddamn it.'

Evander fought against the urge to put his fist through the door. Without another word he very gently, very carefully closed the door. Leaning his head against it, he breathed through the anger and self-recriminations. He looked around the room, the bed a punch to the gut.

He had shirked his obligations and chosen to spend a night with a woman. He let out a breath, no, he wasn't going to regret last night. It had been the most incredible evening and was the first night since the war had ended that he hadn't woken in a cold sweat.

He couldn't regret that.

Something swirled in his stomach and he moved back to

the bed, pulling back the covers, as if the answers lay between the sheets.

There, in the imprint of her body, right where her heart would have been, lay the Faberge egg.

ARIADNE RESTED her hand in the pristine glove of the porter and stepped up into the barren carriage of the funicular.

She made her way to the same bench she had occupied on her way up the mountain. Running her hand slowly across the back of the bench where her broad-shouldered man had sat, she smiled a little to herself. This was not the way she had imagined she would be leaving the Chateau.

Last night had been the most electrifying night of her life, nothing could compare. Not even the first night she and Evander had met on the steps of the Rijksmuseum. He and his team looking for the small, stolen carving of Dionysus and her, standing right behind him, with it in her coat pocket.

She stroked her flat palm lovingly along the front cover of the book in her lap before carefully running her nail along where the front page met the spine. She smiled in delight as the colourless jewels hidden inside the book glinted as the light hit them.

Her client had requested she find and retrieve the expensive brooch that had been taken from his family home by Valentina, his disgruntled lover. A brooch which was now being used to blackmail him into resuming the relationship. A brooch he would pay handsomely to recover, figuring the expense of his divorce would total much, much more.

Once Ariadne had learned the brooch and its wearer were going to be in attendance at a remote mountainside resort with some of the world's most famous (and expensive) artwork as well as the rumoured Faberge egg, she had been unable to resist.

And, she thought, as she drew a heart on the window in the fog left behind by her breath, the opportunity to spend time with the one man she was never able to get close to.

The only man who seemed to understand her, whose intelligence came even close to hers and, she couldn't deny, the man she had been longing for from the first conversation they'd had on the steps of the Rijksmuseum. Her raison d'etre. How she had longed to unleash him. To see how his eyes flashed as he finally let go of the emotion he held so tightly in check. She smiled as the events of the night before came back to her.

The smile faded as her eyes locked with his as he walked out of the hotel's entrance. He stood, stock still, at the top of the steps, his clothes rumpled as if picked up from the floor and donned without thought.

The carriage jolted as it started its journey back down the cliff-side and he took an involuntary step forward. She shivered despite her thick coat and a heaviness she feared she would never shake descended into the pit of her stomach.

For the first time since she had begun her career as the one they called Le Malin Renard she found herself experiencing regret for the choices she had made. She looked at Evander and pain sliced at her heart. Her decisions had led her to him, yes, but they also meant that he would never, *could never*, be hers.

She closed her eyes briefly against the agony of that thought.

She held her palm up to the window.

After what felt like an eternity, he raised his own, bringing it up lightly to his hat.

The carriage dipped over the ledge, down the mountain-side, removing him from her sight completely. She closed her eyes and leaned her head against the cool damp window. The cold of the glass a welcome pain. A pain that might help her think of something other than how empty this victory felt.

She longed to feel the most amazing things, her entire life was dedicated to it. Dedicated to taking risks and experiencing the thrill of planning and executing the most outrageous and daring feats. But she feared she had just lost something irreplaceable at Hotel Lilâ, something worth more than any of the art in the world.

The funicular squealed to a stop without her noticing any part of the journey and she carefully tucked the brooch back into the book, pressing against the crease to reseal it.

The platform was crowded with men in dark capes, all wearing the distinctive flat-topped hats of *la Gendermarie*. The blood rushed through her arms as her gaze met the eyes of the closest policeman, standing at the doorway of the funicular.

She dug her fingers into the mink stole's fur, squeezing tightly to release all the adrenalin flooding her body.

How fast can you run in those shoes?

She smirked as she looked down at her teal alligator pumps, tied with a velvet black ribbon. Le Malin Renard had no need to run.

Time moved in slow motion as she lifted her case and made her towards the door. The young policeman reached his hand to hers from the platform and she held his gaze boldly, placing the tiny little claw of Minky in his hand instead of her own.

His expression shifted from confusion to disgust in an instant as he was greeted by the beady eyes of the stole, showing its sharp, spiked teeth in a wretched smile.

Ariadne grasped his hand firmly with her own before giving him a little wink, smiling as the colour rose in his cheeks.

'Merci,' she said warmly over her shoulder at him as she and the stole walked briskly towards the exit.

A ruby red Rolls Royce Silver Ghost was parked at a jaunty angle near the steps leading from the funicular station and she stepped lightly down the stairs leading toward it, handing her suitcase to the smartly suited chauffeur waiting beside its open door.

Carefully she arranged Minky and her book on her lap, smoothing her skirt against the cool leather seat, as the car took off from the roadside.

She knew he would never stop looking for Le Malin Renard, but now she also knew, Le Malin Renard would never stop looking for him.

St Tropez
Some months later

riadne slid her oversized sunhat off and smoothed her hand along her crimped hair, still surprised by the feel of the closely cropped strands. Whisking the wide leg of her linen pants aside, she tucked her legs under her and closed her eyes against the warmth of the summer sun. Leaning her head against the salt crusted fabric of the daybed, a small sigh escaped.

Day three of waiting.

She had sat in the relentless sun for three months at the entrance of the Louvre, on the same unforgiving wooden bench for hours at a time but that didn't compare to the agony of this wait.

The scents and noise of St Tropez in full swing washed over her, merging into a delightful cacophony of sight and sound. The light of the afternoon sun played and frolicked on the fringe of the beach umbrella, sending patterns and shadows along her closed lids. She tracked their dance lightly until a shadow fell across her face and sang along her skin. She drew in a deep breath, savouring his scent, so undeniably him, even after all this time.

She held her eyes closed a moment, afraid to make the smallest movement. Sniffing the air slightly, she tried to sense if it was one man or twenty waiting for her to open her eyes.

Gathering her mettle, she looked up to see Evander, only Evander standing beside her. Propping herself up on an elbow she shielded her eyes from the sun with an elegant hand, her smile one of unadulterated joy.

Her casual pose was completely affected and she worked desperately to stay seated while every fibre of her being longed to leap from the chair into his arms. Painstakingly she ran her eyes down along his body, cataloguing every tiny detail. From his cream linen trousers to the shirt unbuttoned at his neck. His jacket pushed up at his wrists. His boater hat perched at a jaunty angle.

He looked like a man on holiday.

He sat his brown wicker suitcase down beside her lounger. The very same suitcase he had placed beside her feet on the funicular all those months ago.

'Inspector.'

He gazed at her a long moment before giving a slight shake of his head.

'Le Malin Renard was reported to be killed in a train accident in Switzerland recently,' was all he said.

She widened her eyes before catching her lower lip between her teeth.

It had taken months to find a John Doe case that could pass for Renard. Once she had found the perfect situation (for her—certainly not for poor John Doe!) she had written letters to the French newspapers, who were only too happy to report that the infamous Le Malin Renard had been finally stopped in his tracks. She had spent the months while looking for her John Doe detaching herself from her alias, saying goodbye to the life she had created in the hope that one day they would meet again, could meet again.

'My role was to head up the taskforce designed to catch him. No Renard, no taskforce.'

He gazed out to the azure ocean, the warm salty breeze bringing with it all the pleasures of the seaside; of endless days with little to do but enjoy the exploration of coastal towns, of long, leisurely lunches at cafes beside the water, of lazy mornings spent in a tangle of sheets with your lover.

'So, I resigned. I thought it might be time to take an extended holiday.'

He reached into his jacket pocket and pulled out a well-thumbed postcard, bearing a hand-sketched picture of the exact view from where he stood. She didn't need to look at it to know the numbers written carefully on the back represented the dates she would be here waiting, for she had laboured over them into the early hours of a cold winter's evening.

She sat upright, all thoughts of alluring poses gone from her mind. Reaching for his hand, she entwined her fingers between his. He tugged on her hand lightly, pulling her up from the lounger into his arms. They stood perfectly still for a moment, their eyes locked.

She had known excitement that made her heart beat so hard in her chest it reverberated in her ears, caused her palms to slicken, and at times, had kept her awake, fizzing, all night. But none of it compared to how she felt in this moment.

'I didn't know if you would come,' she said, focussing on the small clear button at the top of his shirt.

He cradled her face between his palms, staring deep into her eyes.

'I couldn't stay away. Renard…' He shook his head, '*you are the other half of me. It is all just so pointless without you.*'

'Renard is dead. Ariadne is all that is left.'

'Ariadne is all I want.'

A wave of relief swept through her and she closed the distance between them, pressing her lips against his. All the months of hot longing and cold doubt disappeared as if the time that had passed hadn't existed at all. She was exactly where she belonged.

Her hands gripped the labels of his jacket, wringing the fabric tightly in her hands to still them from the journey they longed to take.

She nodded out to a wooden sailboat anchored offshore, bobbing gently in the crystal-clear waters.

'That is my boat—*Le Bon Homme*—I was planning to visit the Greek Isles for a spell. Have you ever been to Egypt?'

He narrowed his eyes.

'There will be no plundering on this trip.'

She ran her gaze down his chest, pausing ever so slightly at his belt before raising her dancing eyes back to his.

'What a pity.'

His laugh was a thing of such beauty that the wind ceased to stir, a legion of stars fell from the sky, the swell of the tide shifted and Cupid nudged Eros, where they sat upon the sea wall.

He gestured to the cerulean lounger next to hers.

'Is this seat taken?'

She nodded her head.

'Oui, it is reserved. Pour vous. For ever.'

THE END

EOS

By Clare Griffin

PROLOGUE

Kentucky, USA
Easter Sunday, April 21st, 1946

For months afterwards, the newspapers asked only one thing: what happened to Rosamund Winter?

It had been a nice distraction for the people as the war raged on to gossip and dissect what could have happened to one of America's sweethearts. The weak minded said she never should have been flying planes in the first place. Others thought she was a hero. But the war was over and the American way of life was slowly starting to come back together, piece by piece like a patchwork quilt. Now, three years later people wanted to know what had happened to the brunette bombshell from Kentucky.

Tobias threw the newspaper across the table in disgust, his heart twinging as it did every time her name came up, not that it was often anymore. He picked up his coffee and taking a sip, looked out the window at the rolling green hills just as his eyes settled on a black speck at the top of one of the fields. He squinted with confusion and leant forward as if this small amount of movement would help him identify the stranger on the hill.

'What the hell?' he said aloud as the speck kept moving towards him.

He stood and moved the lace curtain aside, his eyes narrowing against the glare. The speck had now become two figures but they were too far away to ascertain any defining features. There was something familiar about the gait of the taller person: head high, looking forward, long, confident strides. But the other figure walked slowly and not as confidently, the taller one quite often waiting for the second to catch up.

His eyes never leaving the windows, he walked through the front rooms, hurrying, afraid that if he lost sight of the bodies they may disappear. He wrenched the front door open and walked onto the porch. He stopped shy of the steps as his eyes scanned the horizon. The figures were gone. Sighing, he turned to go back inside when he heard a voice float over the breeze. He spun on his heel to identify it but couldn't see anyone. Someone was singing something, but he was only getting every second word as the wind chose what to carry to him.

Walking as if in a trance, he was compelled forward, as if the song was a siren's call and he was being led to his demise, powerless. He had the strange feeling he had been here before, dreamt of this moment, it was familiar yet strange at the same time, like he knew what would happen next. No sooner had the thought flashed into his mind, the figures stopped at the top of the crest, a few metres from the house.

Tobias fell to his knees, air escaping from his mouth in a hiss as if being squeezed out through a vice.

But it couldn't be. Tobias didn't believe in ghosts.

CHAPTER 1

Hollywood, USA
November, 1943

'For the last goddamn time, you are not getting out of your contract to go and fly some goddamn planes across the country. Your face and your ass belong on the screen. *That's* your war effort, sweetheart.'

Jack Warner slammed his fist down on his massive oak desk for the third time but the woman in front of him didn't even flinch.

Rosamund Winter sighed and readjusted the fox fur around her shoulders, crossing and uncrossing her legs. As predicted, the older man's eyes fell to her nylon-clad calves and she barely restrained the urge to roll her eyes. Instead she flicked her thick dark brown tresses over her shoulder and parted her plump lips slightly, inhaling in a way that she knew drove her male audiences wild.

'But Jacky, think of the publicity it will bring the studio...'

'Don't you Jacky me' he said, his eyes now on her mouth.

'Those sweet lips making men stand to attention is what will get this studio publicity.'

This time Rosamund did allow her eyes to roll.

'There!' he said punching the air with his finger. 'There she is, there's my firefly. Under all the sex and sass you're still a little feisty country girl underneath.'

'Says the man who was born in Canada,' she retorted.

Jack Warner leant back in his chair and hooted with laughter. 'Touché sweetheart, touché.'

Rosamund leant forward in her chair so her face was in the full light of his office. She was going to have to give the performance of her life. Her face and body had gotten her to Hollywood, but she had climbed the ranks due to her talent and hard work ethic. Jack Warner had been her big break, as he liked to remind her regularly.

'Jack, the US Government would be very appreciative of you letting me go and fly planes. Promotion aside, think of the money they might fling your way for your help in the war effort.'

Rosamund held her breath as she waited for Jack's response. She had no idea if the Government would give him money, but she knew that if there was one thing Jack Warner loved, it was money. She smiled under hooded lids and readjusted her fur so he copped a hint of her cleavage. The tight burgundy wraparound dress had been chosen specifically for this job, hugging her curves in all the right places. Rosamund didn't like using her body to get what she wanted, but as long as men thought with their pants, she would continue to use her feminine wiles while she could.

She leant on her elbow on the armrest and waited, Jack's eyes appraising her.

'The answer is still no. Now get the hell out of my office.'

Rosamund stood, squaring her shoulders. She started to speak but Jack held up his hand.

'Nothing you say or do will change my mind. You signed a contract with me for seven years. Your ass is mine until you stop making me money. And you know what happens to actresses who refuse to work.'

He smiled at her but the smile didn't meet his eyes. She spun on her heel and opened the door, only to collide with a young woman.

'I'm, oh, I'm so sorry!' the woman said, not meeting Rosamund's eyes. Christ, she thought, she can't be more than fifteen. The girl looked up at Rosamund and gasped.

'You're Rosamund Winter! Oh I'm such a huge fan, you're the reason I wanted to get into movies in the first place! I've seen all your films. I'm so sorry I bumped into you.'

The girl looked as if she was about to cry.

'Never mind, no harm done.'

Rosamund looked the girl over. She could have been a younger, mini version of her. Dark full hair, pretty face with big, full lips. Dark eyes and a petite but curvy figure. They were getting younger.

Rosamund felt Jack come up behind her.

'Trying to recruit Faith to your cause as well, Rosamund?'

Rosamund turned and kissed Jack on each cheek with false sincerity.

'Pleasure as always, Jack.'

She sashayed away from his office.

'I'll see you on set in two weeks!' Jack yelled after her.

Rosamund squeezed her clutch as if it was the only thing holding her up and she blinked back tears of frustration. She placed her sunglasses firmly on her face while internally repeating her motto: never let the bastards see them break you.

SHE WALKED BACK to her car, looking straight ahead but not really seeing. How had the job which had given her her home and her freedom, suddenly become her prison? How would her movies help the war effort? They wouldn't. She knew it. Jack Warner knew it.

And while people died, risking their lives for a greater cause, she would go through the war, pouting and preening like a peacock on the silver screen.

She opened her clutch to pull out her keys and pulled up short when she saw a familiar figure leaning against her car. She smiled.

'Your driver has the day off?' Rosamund teased as she stopped in front of her old friend and once lover.

'It's the only way I can catch you these days. You haven't been returning my calls,' he replied in his soft Southern accent. It was mostly gone, but he hadn't completely become a Westerner. You could take the boy out of Texas, but you couldn't take Texas out of the boy.

She kissed him on the cheek.

'I'm sorry Howard, I've been a bit preoccupied.'

Her eyes moved over him as she assessed his state of dress and mind. She knew it didn't take much for him to get agitated.

'Do you forgive me?'

He smiled and Rosamund relaxed.

'You know I can never stay angry at you. What's on your mind?'

If there was anyone who understood what she wanted to do, it would be Howard.

'Take a girl out to dinner and she'll tell you all about it?'

'Now that might be the best thing I've heard all day.'

'I'll drive,' she said walking to the driver's side of the car. 'You're faster in the air,' she winked. 'I'm faster on the road.'

Howard gave a low chuckle and opened the door on his side.

'You know I don't have a problem with fast women,' he growled and Rosamund rolled her eyes as she revved the engine.

'No, Howard dear, you *do* have a problem with fast women.'

He was about to reply but she took the words right out of his mouth as she pressed her foot down hard on the accelerator and they screeched out of the Warner Brothers parking lot.

'It's why we'll only ever be friends,' she said quietly.

Between his deafness in one ear and the roar of her Alfa Romeo he never heard her.

She loved Howard, she really did, but she loved his mind. She had never met a man with a sharper engineering brain, except maybe his head engineer and friend Tobias Matthews. Neither man had sniggered at her when she told them she could fly, and wanted to fly more. If anything Howard would have dropped down on one knee then and there.

Rosamund sighed as she remembered the night she had seen Ava Gardner leaving his bungalow. The women had shared a look, Rosamund's of shock, Ava's of pity. She had ended it with Howard that night, and as neither had ever really been in love with the other, they had shifted to friends quickly.

Howard didn't want to lose her as a friend as he didn't have many people he could trust, and she didn't want to lose a billionaire who let her fly his planes.

She drove them back to Howard's mansion in Hancock Park, knowing he would have clothes for her to wear in one of his many spare rooms.

As she flicked through the many designer dresses in the wardrobe, she found one that caught her eye. Sliding her fingers down the smooth, cool fabric, she pulled it out to have a better look. It was a pale pink, almost white silk. The neckline was high around her neck, with the bodice fanning out over the hips and in again at the knees. She turned the hanger around to view the rest of the dress and whistled.

The dress was cut around the body, but had no back, starting again at the base of the wearer's spine. The ties were long enough to be tied in a bow to fall down the back in what appeared to be an attempt at modesty. Rosamund snorted. She pulled it off the hanger and over her head, not caring to think of who had worn it before her.

Howard appeared in the doorway and gave a whistle of appreciation.

'Now honey, remind me why we never got married.'

Rosamund walked to the vanity, picked up her lipstick and applied the bright red stain to her lips, meeting his eyes in the mirror.

'Because you couldn't keep it in your pants and I was sick and tired of the carousel of women.'

Howard nodded.

'I should have done right by you.'

He slumped against the doorway, his brow furrowed and she sighed. Rosamund wanted to have a good night. A fun night to take her mind off her own problems.

'Come on sad sack, I'm not here to make you feel guilty. I'm here to drink you dry.'

She walked over to him and slipped her arm through his.

'I'm hungry, can we leave now?'

Howard kissed her on top of her head.

'Sure Rosie, let's go.'

Not many people called her Rosie. But Howard and Tobias were the only people who knew her real name, the two people she spent the most time with. She hadn't been born Rosamund Winter. Rosamund Winter had been created; a fabrication born out of the Hollywood spin machine.

'Rosemary Parker sounds like a milk maid. No, you need something sexy, exotic,' Jack Warner had said on their first meeting, and so, Rosamund Winter was born.

Howard's driver dropped them off at the Coconut Grove where they were met by the flash flash of lightbulbs on cameras. Howard hated the press, as did she, but they both knew that press for both of them was a good thing. For her, the studio would be happy that she was appearing in the gossip rags, and it made him look like the Hollywood player he so longed to be. They smiled as they walked in, but when they were led to a table that was seated for four, Rosamund stopped in her tracks.

'We expecting some of your other girlfriends to join us this evening?'

She raised an eyebrow as the usher pulled her chair out for her.

'Just a couple of the boys, you'll love it Rosie, you'll be the centre of attention.'

He winked at her as he went to drink the glass of milk placed in front of him. She plucked her cigarette case out of her purse, tapping one out. She put it to her lips when a hand holding matches appeared in front of her face. She turned to discover who the hand belonged to and a smile spread across her face, her stomach fluttering. The man struck a match and she took a long drag, leaning back in her chair.

'Are you out for dinner with me,' she turned to Howard and took another drag, 'or is this a business meeting?'

'I'm sorry Rosamund, did he get you out here on false pretences?'

Tobias sat down next to her and flicked his matches onto the table. Rosamund appreciated again how good looking he was. His dark hair and moustache made his blue eyes smoulder. He filled out his jacket in a way that was attractive to her —broad shoulders and chest that narrowed down to slim hips. It was rare to find a man who was smart, kind and a looker, especially in this town. He'd spent hours with her explaining the ins and outs of everything do with a plane, no matter how many questions she asked, he was always patient. Rosamund gave him a genuine smile.

'Well, if you're here it must mean aviation talk and that's okay by me.'

Without asking he poured her a glass of champagne, something Howard had neglected to do, and handed it to her, placing the bottle back on ice.

'So boys, why are we really here?' Rosamund asked as she took a sip.

The fizzy liquid hit her empty stomach with a splash and made her shiver. She leant back in her chair between the two men and took another drag. The men's gaze met over the table. Howard looked like an excited school boy and he leaned forward, motioning for them to do the same.

'I had a little visit from Uncle Sam this week. Seems they want my expertise in the war effort.'

Rosamund's heart sank. Of course they wanted Howard. He was rich and a man, he could give them what they wanted.

'They want me to design a plane that's big enough to transport troops and anything else they need to fly in.'

His eyes were wide with excitement and his smile spread across his face. He looked like a man much younger than his years and Rosamund couldn't help but smile.

'Howard, this is terrific news! What are you thinking?' Tobias asked.

'I'm thinking of calling it "The Hercules" Howard said.

As the two men spoke across her, Rosamund continued to drink and smoke and wished again that she had more control over her fate. She sometimes wondered if she'd mistakenly been put in a woman's body. Sure it was a lot of fun being a woman, but she was living in a world where men made the rules and called the shots and she was merely a decorative ornament.

Perhaps that's why she loved flying so much. In the air it was just her and some man far away when she needed to radio in. She was in control when she flew and there was nothing but blue skies and fluffy white clouds and the drone of the engines. She was in control. She stumped her cigarette out in frustration and noticed that both men had stopped talking and were looking at her.

'What?' she asked, perplexed.

'I asked you what you thought of the name,' Howard said, his face somewhat crestfallen.

'The Hercules sounds wonderful, Howard,' she said smiling brightly, drawing on all her acting skills. 'This is a wonderful opportunity for you.'

Howard grabbed her hand and she noticed Tobias flinch. He readjusted his bow tie and looked over at another table, watching the argument Errol Flynn was starting. As Howard spoke Rosamund couldn't help but compare the two men. Despite their shared love of aviation and wonderful engineering minds, they were chalk and cheese. Where Howard had a different woman on his arm every night, Rosamund struggled to think of a time where she heard Tobias mention a date, and he'd never made a pass at her, much to her annoyance.

Howard stroked her hand and she turned her gaze back to him.

'Rosie, did you hear me? I want you to be one of my test pilots.'

'Howard, I'm tied to Jack, he won't release me for the war effort, he certainly won't release me to test your planes.'

Hurt flashed across Howard's face and he looked like a child who had been told he couldn't play with a toy. Howard didn't hear *no* a lot and when he did, it normally didn't end well for the other person. Rosamund caressed his cheek.

'It's a wonderful opportunity for you, sweetheart, you ought to be very proud.'

At that moment Errol flung himself at a man across his table and as plates and glasses smashed around them, Rosamund lit another cigarette and gazed upwards as she exhaled. She was ready to leave this town. Howard ignored the usual display of masculinity from Errol, slammed his hand on the table and yelled 'I'll buy you out.'

She laughed and took a long drag on her cigarette and looked at Tobias to see if he was also laughing but he was nodding his head.

'Appeal to his hip pocket,' he said. 'Make him an offer he can't refuse.'

Rosamund's head swung between the two men.

'And then where would I work? You're going to buy my contract and give it to who?' She laughed at the notion of it. Tobias held her gaze.

'It would buy you freedom.'

Rosamund looked into Tobias' teal eyes and couldn't help but smile. He was a beautiful man. Women should have been jumping over themselves to get to him, but as long as he was next to Howard, he would never get a look in.

'When I own a studio you will come and work for *me*,' Howard declared as Errol tackled someone else to the ground behind him. 'I'll buy out your contract and you can come and fly planes for *me*.'

Rosamund looked back at Howard, a flutter of excitement low in stomach as a notion came to her.

'Howard, if you can convince Jack to give up my contract,

can I help with the war effort while you're building the Hercules?'

Goosebumps travelled up her arms at the prospect. Could he really make this happen?

'Of course I would come back and help when you were ready.'

'Sure Rosie, sure, let me draw up a contract and get the ball rolling. First of all, I need to convince Jacky boy that money is more important than you.'

He signalled to the waiter currently cleaning up Errol's mess to get another bottle of champagne while Rosamund sat back in her chair and smiled. Jack Warner hated Howard, but he loved money and if he knew she wasn't going straight to another studio it just might work.

She was yet to be meet a man who didn't love money above all else.

*A*fter dinner, Rosamund and Tobias parted ways with Howard, his eye caught by a pretty young woman, and Tobias drove her back to Howard's who had given them permission to fly his plane. She loved flying at night more than day. She liked to imagine she was flying in space, slicing through the stars. The many lights below them made the dirty city of Los Angeles seem pretty. She loved the shudder of the plane underneath her hands, and how with a slight turn of her wrists, they would turn and circle over the ground below.

'You're never more beautiful than when you fly,' Tobias said. 'You get this… look on your face, a childlike grin that never leaves your face.'

Rosamund looked out the side window and turned the plane, leaning the control stick left.

'I think it's the only time I'm truly happy,' she said, her grin widening.

'Because it's the only time you're totally in control,' and the smile melted off her face. She clamped her mouth shut and stared ahead. She hated that he was right. She was in control, but it was so much more than that. She lived a life where men told her what to eat, what to wear, even who to date. When she was in the sky, there was no one calling the shots except her. No matter what the elements or situation, if she was the pilot, she called the shots.

'Did you always want to fly?' he asked and her grin came back.

'For as long as I can remember, I've always looked to the stars. If I could fly to the moon I would, but until that day, flying in the air is the second best thing. What about you?'

He leant back in his seat and crossed his ankles.

'My father wanted me to be a farmer. My father is a farmer, my father's father was a farmer and so on. Being good at maths and wanting to fly were not two skills I needed or wanted. But we're born as we are.'

Rosamund cast him a side-eyed glance. He looked calm on the outside, his hair and moustache perfectly trimmed, his shirt sleeves rolled up his his elbows, his bow tie opened and hanging around his neck, but his tone was sad. They'd only ever had conversations about planes and engineering in the past, and she was enjoying him letting his guard down.

'Do you see your family very often?' she asked. He sighed and played with the ends of his bow tie, avoiding her gaze.

'I haven't been home in a while,' he said quietly. 'What about you? Where does Rosamund Winter come from?'

'Well, Rosamund Winter was born in Jack Warner's office. Rosemary Parker was Kentucky born and raised.'

Tobias leant over his armrest to look at her more closely, a wry smile upon his lips.

'You hide that well, Miss Parker, I thought you were an East coast girl for sure, not a Southerner.'

Rosamund battered her eyelashes and spoke like a Southern belle.

'I will remind you that I am an actress, Mr Matthews, it is my job to play make believe.'

He laughed and she changed the direction of the plane.

'I bought a big old farmhouse down there for when the studios have had enough of me. I plan to buy my own small plane and just fly around my farm, keep some horses and a few chickens. A simple life. A quiet life. But that must sound stupid to you.'

She looked over her shoulder to find his intense gaze on her and her pulse quickened.

'It sounds like the way life should be lived,' and he held her gaze unblinking.

Her skin flushed and her hands slid down the control stick sending the plane downwards. They both lunged for the control panel but Rosamund corrected the flight path, clearing her throat in embarrassment.

'I think the champagne may have caught up with me. Perhaps you should land,' she said, pretending it was the champagne bringing heat to her cheeks and not Tobias.

'Are you sure? Are you okay?' He was by her side now, his hand on her forehead and she laughed.

'I'm not sick Tobias, I'm a little bit tipsy. Trying to convince Warner's to release me has left me a trifle shattered.'

She inhaled and his scent of leather and wood hit her nostrils and she was now lightheaded for another reason. All the blood was leaving her head and pooling a little lower.

'I'll be fine, but you should land her.'

He stood up leaning over her, ready to take the control stick and his hands covered hers.

'When you're ready,' he said and their eyes locked. After a moment he smiled.

'I'm really enjoying holding hands, but it's going to be a little hard to land the plane while I lean over you.'

Rosamund shook her head as if in a daze.

'Sorry, of course, hang on,' and she tried to slide out from under him, the dress making it easy to slide along his back and out of the pilot's seat.

She went and sat in the adjacent seat, her cheeks feeling as if they had been exposed to the sun for hours and she pressed her cheek against the cool glass to try and calm herself. What had come over her?

'I'll take us back to Howard's now.'

Rosamund nodded, not trusting herself to say anything. They were both silent, the rumble of the engines the only noise. Rosamund was lulling into sleep when Tobias' words struck her.

'Have you heard of a lady called Jackie Cochran?'

She sat up in her chair, suddenly very alert.

'Of course I have, she still holds the world speed record for a pilot, male or female and she's an important member of the 99s. Why?'

'She's just come back from England where she was flying with the British Air Transport Auxiliary and she's recruiting female pilots here, as per her suggestion and the request of none other than Mr Franklin D Roosevelt himself.'

Rosamund felt her eyes go wide and she leant towards him, poised to spring, the excitement starting to bubble in her veins.

'She knew of my connection with Howard and she assumed Hollywood was such a small place that I must know you. I told her she was correct. She's apparently been trying to get in contact with you but the studio has obviously not been passing on the messages.'

'No, I haven't heard a thing! Why was she asking after me?'

His smile turned into a wide grin and he locked eyes with her, his eyes vibrant.

'That's the best bit, she wants you to join her down in Texas. She wants to speak to you first, but she's had her eye on you for a while. She's been looking up the flight records of female pilots all over the country and has hand-picked the first class.'

Rosamund's heart thundered under her ribs and she was sure Tobias could hear it over the roar of the engines. This was exactly what she wanted, and now, she wouldn't have to leave the country to do it.

'So, what do you think?' Tobias asked as he began bringing the plane down to land.

'I think that's the best bit of news I've heard in a long time.'

As he brought the plane down smoothly on the tarmac, Rosamund's mind raced. She was so close to making a difference, so close, but she just had to remove one big obstacle first.

JACK'S FACE was thunderous when he saw who had accompanied Rosamund to his office. He had his hand on the phone receiver to call security when Howard slid a piece of paper across Jack's desk.

'Can you count that many zeroes Jacky?' Howard drawled.

Rosamund sat in the same chair she had been seated in the day before and lit a cigarette. On the outside she looked like a woman in control, a woman without a care in the world, but on the inside, she was a hurricane of fear. If this didn't work, it just might anger Jack Warner enough to keep her on contract but not offer her any roles: no work and no flying of planes.

Howard sat next to Rosamund but didn't look at her. He

was in business mode; for Howard this was just another business transaction, no feelings or emotions involved, even though he was essentially buying her.

'What is this?' Jack asked creaking down in his chair, his arms crossed over his chest, his hands tucked under each armpit. He pushed the paper away from him as if it was a piece of trash. He looked down his nose at Rosamund. 'Run straight to money bags did you?'

Rosamund narrowed her eyes and took a drag of her cigarette.

'Actually, he came to me.'

'Do you like what you see?' Howard asked getting impatient. 'I want to buy out Miss Winter's contract and that's how much I'll pay you for it. I think you'll agree it's a fair sum.'

Jack sniggered. 'It's a ridiculous figure! Ludicrous! You want to spend this much on her? And then what? Where will she work? Which studio are you taking her to?'

'Does it matter where I go, Jack? You said it yourself, apparently I'm not worth the money.'

Rosamund took another drag and tilted her head waiting. Her heart hammered against her ribs and she was sure the two men could hear it. Jack cast his eyes downward and looked at the figure again as if he couldn't quite believe his eyes.

'She's a bad investment. I can't imagine your little tool board will be happy you're spending this much money on an actress that will probably get knocked up and ruin her figure. She's entering her twilight years,' Jack said, his eyes boring into Rosamund.

'She's twenty-three,' Howard said, probably annoyed this meeting was taking longer than he expected.

'Exactly, plenty of women years younger than her on our books just waiting for their chance.'

Rosamund smiled, her heart rate slowly dropping. She watched as Jack's eyes kept darting back to the paper Howard had given him, and she knew he was torn. He wasn't saying this about Rosamund to be mean, he was trying to talk Howard out of it. He was going to say yes to the money, but she knew he didn't want to lose her.

'Jack, we've been through a lot together,' Rosamund started. 'I'll always be grateful for everything you've done for me. I owe my career to you and this studio and I leave with a heavy heart.' Jack looked up at her, his eyes cold, but she knew it was a front. 'You can put it into the contract that I won't work for another studio for a year.'

'Two,' he said not missing a beat and Rosamund pursed her lips. Two years not working was a long time. The war would most likely be over soon and then what would she do? Howard wouldn't pay her to fly planes. Jack did have a point, she wasn't getting any younger and by the time she would be able to work again she'd be twenty-five.

'Rosie, two years will *fly* by,' Howard said and the emphasis on the word fly wasn't lost on her. She stood and walked to Jack's side of the desk and kissed him on each cheek. He caught her hands and gave them a squeeze.

'You sure you know what you're doing, kid?' he asked her and she nodded. 'Well, I'm gonna miss your spunk.'

'No, you won't,' she laughed, fighting the urge to cry and pulling her hands out of his.

'You'll be thrilled to replace me with someone who can't think for themselves and will only say "Yes Jack, whatever you say, Jack".'

He laughed and sat back.

'Good luck to you, Rosemary Parker. Let me talk business with tool man here. I look forward to seeing what you do next.' He smiled at her and for the first time since she'd signed her contract with Warner Brothers, the smile met his eyes.

'Goodbye Jack.'

She nodded at Howard and left the men to decide her leaving price. For the first time in years, she breathed deeply and lightly. A weight had been lifted off her shoulders.

She was free.

HOWARD FOUND her floating in her pool at home. Her eyes were closed behind winged sunglasses, her face tilted towards the Californian sun, the water bobbing her around. She knew it was Howard from the hurried, impatient gait on the patio tiles. It was the second pair of footsteps that made her lift her glasses to see who was with him. When her eyes fell on Tobias she was glad she had decided to wear a costume and not go nude as she often liked to.

'You're free Rosie. My people have drawn up an agreement and wired the funds over to Warner Brothers, and you are officially unemployed. Congratulations.'

Rosamund swum to the side of the pool and lifted up her sunglasses.

'I'd say this calls for drinks,' she said, about to lift herself out, but Howard shook his head and she sunk back into the cool water.

'I've got to get back to the office and keep working on the Hercules. Congratulations again, Rosie. I expect you to be available when I need you. Tobias here will bring you up to speed.'

He turned on his heel and left and Rosamund shook her head laughing.

'The ever-effable Mr Hughes, ladies and gentlemen,' Rosamund said, shaking her head as she pressed her feet against the side of the pool to shoot herself backwards through the water.

'I bet he already has a schedule drawn up for me, doesn't he?'

Tobias sat down on one of the deck chairs to loosen his tie and throw it on the table. He spoke as he rolled up his sleeves.

'I hope you're aware you've swapped one master for another. Howard is planning on using you as part of his marketing campaign. He's already making sketches of the outfit you'll wear while flying.'

Rosamund rolled her eyes and dunked her head under. For a moment everything disappeared as her ears fell under the water line, the only sound the warped water moving against the side of the pool.

She pulled her head back out of the water.

'I can imagine. What do you need to tell me?'

She swum back over to the side of the pool towards the steps. She could feel his eyes on her but she pretended he wasn't watching. She bent over to pick up her towel and cast her eyes to the left where he sat. Hidden behind her glasses she watched as his eyes fell over her body lines and she shivered.

'Why don't you get in and cool off? I'm sure I have some trunks here you can wear,' she said, waving towards the house. He undid three buttons on his shirt and Rosamund looked away. This was the most she had seen him undressed and it was causing a strong reaction in her, much stronger than it should. Her lips parted as her skin flushed. She watched as he moved his hands backwards and forwards across his thighs and she wondered what his hands would feel like on her.

'Thanks, but I won't be here long.' A heavy fist of disappointment hit her and she shook her head as if to rid herself of the feeling. 'I have a dinner date.'

'Oh?' she said barely keeping the disappointment out of her voice. 'Who's the lucky lady?'

Tobias smiled.

'Dicky Carter. He insists on meeting me at the Grove.'

Rosamund laughed.

'Lucky you,' she said tying a peach-coloured dressing gown around her wet body. Dicky was one of Howard's right hand men and no doubt it would be a boring dinner.

'All I want to do is stay hidden in the hangar, go over the designs with Howard, but I'm being sent to these meetings more and more.'

'Have you told Howard how you feel?' He gave her a look and Rosamund put her hands up. 'Fair enough, I know how much he loves to hear the word no.'

She leant over to pour herself a glass of her heavily laced iced tea and held the jug up to Tobias. He shook his head and she replaced it. 'When will you be in the hangar next?'

'I'm hoping tomorrow morning, dawn flight.'

Rosamund sat up straighter.

'Can I come?' she asked.

'If you lay off those you can come up,' he said pointing at her baller glass. She put it down and tucked her feet underneath her.

'Righto boss,' she said saluting him.

'Be at the hangar at 0500 hours,' he said winking.

CHAPTER 3

Rosamund arrived at four thirty, the sky still dark, the soft pinks of sunrise barely peeking through the dark clouds. She parked her car in front of the hangar, her heart racing. She pulled the scarf off her hair and shook her waves out. This is what made her feel alive. She stepped out of the car and immediately was hit with the smell of engine fuel and oil and she smiled: some women loved perfume, she loved aviation fuel.

She walked around the trunk of her car and pulled out her small leather bag. The square satchel contained everything she needed to fly: her goggles, gloves and a compass. She walked over to the hangar door and squeezed through the gap.

Tobias ran his hand underneath the body of a small plane, his lips pursed in concentration. She didn't want to disturb him so she attempted to creep along the wall in the shadows.

'Just as well you can act because you're not light enough on your feet to be a dancer,' he said, never taking his eyes off the plane. She watched as his fingers glided over the sleek pressed metal with the care and precision of a surgeon.

Rosamund smiled but made her answer sound like she was offended.

'You calling me plump, Mr Matthews? It's not nice to comment on a woman's weight or age.'

'I'm saying you're not very light on your feet.'

His eyes moved to her then and his smile was warm. She stepped out of the shadows and beamed right back.

'You're early. You know the army like you to follow rules, arriving early is just as bad as arriving late.'

Rosamund tuck her hands into her leather jacket pockets, the cool morning making her shiver.

'I'm sorry Tobias, I didn't realize you'd gone and joined the army overnight. I'll just go back to my car and come back at 0500 sharp...' she turned to walk away but he didn't say anything and she stopped.

'What are you doing anyway? Isn't that Howard's plane?'

Tobias sighed and pulled a rag out of his pant pockets and rubbed his hands.

'Yeah it is. He's planning on flying to Houston today to explain to the board why he spent so much money on an actress.'

'That news got to them fast,' she said.

Tobias shrugged. 'He's watched like a hawk when he's in Hollywood, even more so in Texas which is why he spends so much time here. He is the company but the board still regulate how he can spend his money. This is why he's so excited to be working for the government. Hughes Tools can't touch it.' He pushed the rag into the back pocket of his overalls and stepped towards her. His head dipped as he lifted his eyes towards her.

'He knows you're a damn fine pilot though. Don't worry, you won't need to go back to Warner.'

Rosamund smiled. 'Thanks Tobias.'

He shrugged. 'I don't think it matters what you have

between your legs as long as you can fly.' He nodded for her to follow and they walked further into the hangar. 'I've got a surprise for you. If you really want to fly for the army, you're going to be flying two and four engines, bigger and heavier then you've even flown before. You've got the hours, but let's show them you've got the stuff.'

He blushed and Rosamund looked at him quizzically.

'Whatever is the matter?'

Tobias cleared his throat and stroked his moustache nervously, looking everywhere but her face. Rosamund moved towards him and doing so, stepped back into the light. His eyes were dark but she couldn't tell if he was angry or upset.

'You know I think you're a great pilot, better than some of the men I know.'

'Thank you, yes I know, women do a lot of things better than men,' she said, lightly trying to ease the tension.

'But I need to prepare you. I know you're tough, you're one of the strongest willed and hardest working people I've met. But Jackie's got her work cut out for her. This is the Army Air Force we're talking about. They're not going to think this will work.'

Rosamund raised her eyebrows in disbelief.

'But it's working in England right now. Surely they don't think British women are better equipped than Americans?'

'I don't think most men would think any woman are equipped to fly a plane, British or American.'

'But not you. You've never had a problem with me flying. Why is that?'

She stepped closer to him so that they were only inches away from each other. Her forehead only came to his chest and she had to crick her neck to look up at him. She breathed him in; his scent was leather…and spice, natural masculine smell. His shirt and coveralls were rolled up to his elbows, his three top buttons not done up like the day before. She was so close she could count the stubble on his chin. His moustache was perfectly groomed but he'd obviously forgotten to shave that morning. Something passed over his face but she couldn't place what it was.

'You've never given me a reason to doubt your ability.'

A smile spread across her lips.

'But I'm a woman, flighty, nervous, high strung,' she said with mock seriousness.

'I've heard you called worse,' he said. He went to put his hand towards her face, but at the last minute moved it back over his hair instead. 'Come on. Let me show you your surprise.'

He spun on his heel and ducked under the plane he'd been looking over. Rosamund didn't follow him right away, assessing what she was feeling. She found she was disappointed he hadn't touched her, her stomach heavy with the feeling as she moved her hand to where his should have gone. She followed Tobias, weaving and ducking under planes and gasped when she found him standing next to a huge four engine B17.

'How in the world…?' Rosamund said her voice breaking. 'How did you get this?'

She walked towards the plane and ran her fingers across the sleek metal body. She ran her hand over the engines, imagining the power they must create. She looked back to Tobias who had a goofy look on his face, his mouth open and smiling, clearly proud of his surprise.

'A pal of mine is in the Army Air Force and wanted me to take a look at the plane. She was a bit banged up when she came in but she's as good as gold now. I thought you might like to have a go. Then when you head off to Jackie you can tell her you've flown a B17.'

Rosamund ran towards him and wrapped her arms around his neck.

'Thank you, thank you, thank you!' She squealed like a schoolgirl. 'You don't know how much this means to me.' She added a peck on his cheek before she ran towards the left hand side of the plane but still she heard his words spoken softly.

'I think I do.'

~

Rosamund ground to a halt when she reached the side of the plane.

'Say Tobias, how is a girl supposed to get up there?'

When she stretched out on tippy toes, her fingers barely reached the body of the plane.

'Dammit,' she muttered. 'I'm taller than most of the actresses on the lot. How are most women going to even get into these?' She tapped her foot in concentration. 'If we use ladders they'll laugh us right out of the army.'

'One thing at a time, cowgirl,' Tobias said grinning. He walked up behind her and pointed over her shoulder. 'There's a door there,' his breath warm on her cheek. Her eyes followed his arm and found a tiny door almost underneath the plane.

'You're joking,' she said. 'It looks like it's been designed for circus midgets.' They walked towards the door which Tobias opened and pulled out a narrow step ladder. Rosamund raised up on her toes and stuck her head up into the cavernous plane, her heart racing with excitement. She felt Tobias move next to her and their arms brushed. She flinched as if she'd been shocked and goosebumps appeared on her arms, her heart jolting now for a different reason.

'Ladies first.'

She climbed the ladder, taking tiny movements up the steep steps. She stopped when she stepped into the body of the plane, having never seen anything like it. She'd never been in a pursuit plane before and she tried to take everything in at once: bomb bay, machine guns, wooden desk with a chair and lamp. The plane seemed to go on forever as she stood in the middle. Every part of the plane had a purpose and no space was spared.

She hadn't moved far enough into the body of the plane and Tobias bumped into her knocking her forward, but caught her around the waist before she fell.

'Sorry!'

'I'm so sorry,' they said at the same time. They stood up but neither moved, Tobias' arm still wrapped around her. She could feel his heart thundering into her back. She turned her head against his chest and he pressed his face to her head.

'I...' Tobias began but Howard's yelling across the hangar made them both jump apart.

'We better get going. You start her up, but I'll drive her onto the runway and then you can do some practice take offs and landings.'

Rosamund could only nod, her pulse racing. She followed him to the cockpit and her eyes went wide.

The two pilot seats reclined slightly, seated close together with barely an inch worth of padding; they were made for practicality, not comfort. The seats were crammed in amongst instruments, dials and levers in front, in between and next to both seats. She took her seat on the left and wrapped her fingers around the gear stick, grinning.

Tobias ran her through some of the dials and levers she'd not seen before and she started her up. She watched as the first engine spluttered into life, the smoke from the oil whirring out the back then clearing once it got going. Once engine one was going she repeated the task three more times.

The roar of the four engines reverberated to her core and her pulse quickened with joy, the grin spread across her face.

Tobias taxied her to the runway and ran her through some directions. She went to press on the pedals to move the rudder when she tapped air. Confused, she looked down to discover she was a foot too far away from the pedals.

'Oh you've got to be kidding,' she said slamming her head back against the seat in frustration. Tobias said nothing but bent forward and pulled a box out from under his seat. Rosamund looked at him, amused.

'There some kind of magic potion in there that will make me taller?' she joked, taking the box from him.

She removed the lid to discover cream tissue paper. Underneath were two wooden blocks with ropes cut into them. 'You really know how to flatter a girl, but I don't understand.'

Tobias got out of his seat and knelt next to her chair.

'They're for your feet. I guessed this may be a problem so I made you some blocks. I'm happy to make more if you find other ladies have the same issues.'

Rosamund shook her head in amazement.

'You really have thought of everything, haven't you?'

Tobias shrugged as if it was nothing and indicated towards the panel.

'Take her up Miss Winter.'

Rosamund slipped the blocks underneath her feet and fastened the rope so they were locked in place. She then moved the rudder to test.

'They work beautifully!'

She did her final checks and then they began to roll. The power of the B17 shocked her, the thrust slamming her back against the seat and she had to concentrate to keep her straight. Her arms were taunt with pressure from the weight of the plane. As they picked up speed the plane began to shudder.

'That's perfectly normal, she's a big girl, she needs a lot of thrust.'

Rosamund's hands shook on the gear stick as she pulled it back towards her. They began to ascend.

'Well done Rosie, well done!' He clapped her on the back and she smiled with relief and pride.

'That's the first time you've called me Rosie.' She watched him out of the corner of her eye. 'That's ok, you can call me Rosie.'

She turned to smile at him and he returned it with a small grin.

'Make a circle then take her down to land and we'll do this all again.'

Rosamund circled the area, marvelling as she did every time at how small everything looked below. The drone of the engines soothed her nerves, but after a few take offs and landings her arms tired, although she didn't want to admit it. Tobias, as if reading her mind, or perhaps noticing her fatigue, instructed her to have a fly around.

The sun was now rising and cast the sky in pinks and mauves. She tilted the stick to the left and they circled over the Hollywood sign.

'Let me see if I can find your house,' she said and winked. Taking in the view, they enjoyed a few moments of silence.

'Have you ever heard of Eos?' Tobias asked. Rosamund shook her head as she looked out the window.

'I think that's Jack Warner's place. Too bad planes don't have horns,' she joked. 'What is Eos?'

'You mean *who* is Eos. According to the Greeks she is the goddess of the dawn. She is one of the Titan goddesses and she is the reason the sun rises every morning. In the writings and paintings she is described as rosy and golden. This light on your face reminds me of her.'

Rosamund looked at him as he continued.

'She's also the mother of the Anemoi.'

'The Ane-whatsit?'

'The Anemoi are the four winds.' Tobias kept his gaze on her and held up his fingers, counting. 'Boreus, the north wind, Notus the south, Zephyrus the west and Eurus...'

'The east wind,' Rosamund finished. 'But what has this...'

Tobias leant over so he was inches from her face.

'You've been called worse,' he said and stopped just shy of her face.

'A Greek goddess is hardly an insult,' she said breathlessly. He moved towards her and gently pressed his mouth to hers. She leant forward so their lips crushed against each other, and for a moment, they remained unmoving. Tobias pulled away and Rosamund bit her lip.

'Land the plane and then I can kiss you like I want to.'

She grinned and turned the plane to the right, knocking him back into his seat.

'Hold onto that thought because I'm not ready to come down just yet.'

By the time she landed, Rosamund's arms were shaking. Keeping the plane under control in the air took a tremendous amount of strength. She was glad she had got to experience the flight with a friend and not a military instructor. Friend. Was that what Tobias was now? Or was he something else?

He helped her down from the cockpit and they walked towards her car.

'I can give you a lift if you like.'

'How about I give you a lift?' she said passing his coupe and heading towards her car. She unlocked the trunk and threw in her bag. Closing the lid, she lent on the back of her car, locking her ankles casually, arms crossed.

'Well? Are you getting in?' she purred, biting her bottom lip.

Tobias smiled and dropped his bag at her feet. 'I've heard a lot about your driving, none of it good.'

'The only people that criticise my driving are the ones that can't keep up.' She smirked at him. 'I think you could keep up.'

Tobias slowly walked towards her and leant forwards so he was close to her face. Before he could speak one of the mechanics ran out yelling Rosamund's name. She held Tobias' gaze, hoping he would ignore the gesticulating mechanic, but it was too late.

'I'm sorry to disturb you, Miss Winter, Toby,' he said his cheeks flushed. 'But there's a Mrs Cochran on the phone for you and she said she's not getting off the phone until she speaks to you. And Mr Hughes is about to leave for Houston and he's getting mighty mad she's holding up the phone line.'

Rosamund looked at Tobias.

'How does Jackie Cochran know where I am?'

Tobias grinned, a grin that made Rosamund want to grab him and make him finish what he'd started.

'You'll soon learn that nothing comes between Jackie Cochran and what she wants.'

She followed the mechanic inside but Tobias didn't follow and she stopped.

'Are you coming in?'

He ground his heel into the earth. 'No, you go.'

'Will you come to dinner? At mine?'

The mechanic was now fidgeting by her side tapping his leg.

'Tonight?'

Howard's bellowing voice floated out to them from the hangar.

'Miss Winter please, if you will…' she popped up her hand to silence him. Tobias opened his mouth as his eyes flickered to something behind her and he clamped his mouth shut. Rosamund spun on her heel to see Howard storming towards them.

'Did he not tell you there's a telephone call? Or was he too star struck to get the words out?'

The poor mechanic shrank in stature and Rosamund felt a pang of regret for not listening to him.

'Howard, please calm down, he did pass the message to me and I was just coming in. I…'

'That woman is holding up the line and I need to make a call. I'm not your damn secretary.'

He loomed over her but Rosamund huffed, pushed past him and walked towards the hangar.

'Thank you, boys, I'll take it from here.'

Howard followed her but she shut the door, leaving him on the other side.

'Hello, Rosamund Winter speaking.'

'Rosamund, you're a hard woman to contact. It's Jackie Cochran.'

'Hello Jackie, Tobias mentioned you've been trying to find me.'

'It's because of him that I knew where you were. It's harder to get through Warner Brothers then getting to speak to Roosevelt.'

Rosamund laughed, glad that she had someone like Tobias on her side.

'Well, Roosevelt probably cares about your amazing aviation feats, while the Warner brothers couldn't give two hoots.'

'Oh they would have if I was about 15 years younger.'

'Touché. How can I help you, Jackie?'

'I'm going to cut right to the chase. I want you. I've been in England working with the women in the British Air Transport Auxiliary, flying all kinds of planes. I'm back Stateside now and I'm starting a program for female pilots to help with the war effort. I've been contacting pilots from all over the country and you were top of my list. If it wasn't for Tobias I have no idea how I would have gotten to you.'

Rosamund's heart rate spiked. 'What's the program you're running here in the States?'

'I've been given the greenlight to start teaching women who already have a pilot's licence to fly military planes around the country. By having women in the skies, it will mean that the men are free to go to the combat roles. So, what do you think?'

'I think it's a great idea. Count me in!'

'I was hoping you'd say that. And Rosamund?'

'Yes?'

'Just a heads up—by you doing this, we are likely to attract a lot of attention. I need you to understand that I can't have any controversy or scandal being connected to this program and my girls. I need pilots to fly like men, but act like ladies outside of the cockpit. Do you get my meaning?'

Rosamund's eye's fell on the shadow of a man outside the door and knew it was Howard, trying to eavesdrop, no doubt.

'Yes, Jackie, I know what you mean.'

'Good, because you're a damn good pilot and I need women like you. Tobias assures me that you're not a typical Hollywood actress. You clearly have brains for starters.'

Rosamund bristled at the assumption that all actresses were only good for two things: getting their lines right and lying flat on their backs.

'I'll have you know that Hedy Lamarr is one of the most intelligent women I've ever met, and she's a scientist and inventor as well as an actress.'

'Can she fly a plane?' Jackie shot back without missing a beat.

Rosamund chuckled. 'I bet she could, but I'm not aware that she has.'

'Damn shame. Have you got a pencil?'

Jackie advised her of the address of where she'd be

training and a motel where she could stay and hung up the phone. Howard came in as if it was just good timing and not that he'd been listening the whole time.

'So, you're getting your wish then? Going to become a taxi driver of the sky?'

Rosamund sat down in Howard's chair, the early flight and now this news completely wiping her out.

'Yes, it appears I am. Can I catch a lift to Houston?'

'Houston?' Howard said his eyebrows arching.

'Yes, that's where our training will be based.'

'I suppose so. But I'm flying.'

She rolled her eyes and got up out of her chair.

'Of course Howard, it'll give me a chance to catch up on my beauty sleep. I'll go home and pack and be back within the hour.'

He mumbled something with a nod and went to look at some papers spread across his desk.

She closed the door behind her and almost bumped into the mechanic from earlier.

'Where can I find Tobias?' she asked, her eyes roaming around the hangar, eager to tell him her news.

'Oh, he's gone,' the man sputtered nervously. 'But he said to tell you thank you, but the answer is no.'

He scurried away and Rosamund's shoulders slumped. She didn't know when she'd see him again.

THEY LEFT for Houston that afternoon. Howard offered for her to stay at his mansion in Houston but she politely declined. She hoped it never got back to Jackie that she'd gotten there via Howard in the first place. Jackie had been very clear: any connection with Howard Hughes meant scandal. In her simple dress of white skirt and baby blue blouse, she didn't scream movie star, and she wanted to keep it that way for as long as possible.

She arrived at the training centre which was a huge shed converted into a classroom. They walked into a room with tables and chairs and Rosamund was taken back to her school days. The women took their seats and looked around. The American flag in all her glory was hung up the front next to a crucifix.

A large door to the side of the room was flung open and Jackie Cochran walked through. Her face was the perfect advertisement for her makeup company. She was immaculately made up and dressed in a dark green skirt and white jumper. The shirt underneath was a lighter green and Rosamund couldn't help but think it was a very fashionable take on an army uniform. Her blonde hair was coiffed to perfection.

The women broke out into applause and a few wolf-whistled. Rosamund took the chance to have a better look at her fellow pilots. Most were young, some dressed in designer labels, others wore what Rosamund guessed was their one good outfit. All were excited.

Jackie waved her hands to shush them.

'Thank you, ladies, thank you, but it should be me thanking you. You are the first twenty-eight female pilots in this country and make no mistake, no matter where every woman here has come from, she is one hell of a pilot.'

Rosamund could feel her skin prickle under the gaze of those around her. Whispers of *Hollywood* and *actress* fell on her ears. She straightened her shoulders and focused on Jackie. She'd get rid of their doubt once in the skies.

'I don't think I need to tell you that what we're doing is unprecedented. No one thinks we'll be able to do it. Most people think women shouldn't even be flying planes, that we *can't* fly planes.' A few sniggers went around the room.

'We know we can fly planes, we're all proof of that. I have looked at every single one of your flight records. You have been handpicked by me for this very important job. To help our boys defend the great country that is the United States.'

As she spoke she moved around the room making eye contact with every woman there. Rosamund shivered. This was going to be history in the making.

'You will be flying bigger and newer planes then you ever have before,' Jackie continued. 'Everyone's eyes are on us.' She looked down at her clasped hands, sighed deeply, then looked back up at the women.

'I feel I need to warn you that we are most likely to be judged harsher than our male counterparts. I want you to be a man in the cockpit, but a lady the minute you step out of that plane. Not one scrap of scandal can surround this group. We are here to do a job and our job only. Save your romance for after the war.'

A woman behind Rosamund snorted.

'Do they say this to the fly boys?' she sniggered under her breath.

Rosamund turned around see who had spoken. The woman was tall and striking with the brightest red hair Rosamund had ever seen. She winked at Rosamund, a crooked smile and Rosamund tried not to laugh.

'You will be the first class called the WASPs: Women Airforce Service Pilots,' Jackie continued, and the group twittered.

As Jackie finished her speech, she advised them that there was a motel for those who could afford it, or families willing to put them up for their time in training. She told them to be back at the airfield by 0600 the next day and to make sure they got a good night's sleep. As the women clapped and walked towards Jackie, the redhead sidled up next to Rosamund.

'Now, how the hell did those Warner brothers let an asset like you go?'

Her accent was Southern and as thick as molasses but her perfume was Chanel and her clothes were French designed and cut. Everything about this woman screamed money.

'A whole lot of cash,' Rosamund smiled and the woman threw back her head and hooted, loud and throaty. Rosamund warmed to her immediately.

The woman held out her hand.

'Pearl Sheppard,' she said as Rosamund shook her hand. 'No need to tell me who you are, just let me know what you'd prefer to be called. Her Majesty, perhaps?' She laughed again and Rosamund joined her.

'Rosie will do just fine.'

'Well Rosie, I think we're in for a hell of a time. I'm guessing you'll be joining me at the shack they call a motel?' Rosamund nodded. 'Then let's go. I've got my car out front. How do you feel about dogs?'

The women began to make their way towards the front of the building.

'Ah, I don't not like them, why do you…'

Rosamund stopped dead in her tracks and a woman behind her bumped into her. Everyone stopped and stared at the bright red Jaguar which had two giant Alsatians hanging out of the car. They had red bows in their hair near their ears and took up the driver and passenger seats. Pearl whistled and the two dogs jumped into the back seat and sat obediently.

'Ladies, meet Eleanor and Martha, two of my finest Alsatians and blue ribbon champions. Rosie, shall we?'

Rosamund stared agog at the two dogs. They looked clean but they were huge. She wasn't scared of dogs but she wasn't too keen on jumping in a car with them.

A woman came up next to her. 'I'd do what she asks, or

she might feed you to those things she calls dogs. I've seen horses smaller than those two.'

'Anyone else want a lift?' Pearl asked. 'Plenty of room. I can make the girls move over.'

No one moved or said a word and Rosamund stepped forward.

'Thatta girl Hollywood, the sooner we leave here the sooner we can get a drink.'

Rosamund threw her bags in the trunk and hopped in the car. Pearl made a strange sound and the two dogs dropped down on the seat.

'That's a neat trick. Does it work on men as well?' Rosamund joked as Pearl started the car.

'Ask my three ex-husbands. Never met a man that was worth even a quarter of my dogs. Dogs are the loyalist things in the world and no man has ever been as devoted.'

Pearl popped open the glove box and handed her a head scarf.

'Nothing like Texas dirt. We'll be red by the time we get to the motel but I like the open air.'

Rosamund tied the cream scarf over her hair, put her sunglasses on. As they made their way down the dirt road, red dust curled and swirled around the car. The road was flat like the fields on either side, except for the massive airfield that was coming up on their left. Ellington Airfield was where the AAF were training hundreds of pilots.

'Do you think we'll be flying with the men?' Rosamund yelled over the noise of the road and engine.

'Highly doubt it. I distinctly got the impression we're on our own. The military don't want us and everyone else believes women should be the passengers, not the pilots. We've got our work cut out for us, Hollywood.'

They arrived at the motel and hopped out to check in.

The women agreed to freshen up and meet in Pearl's room for a drink.

'I have the good stuff, better than anything else they'll have in this backwater place.'

Rosamund was led to her room by a very bashful young girl and after thanking and signing an autograph for her, sat down on her bed and sighed. She was longing for a bath and already missed the California sun. Pearl hadn't been joking about the dirt, as she ran her tongue over her gums and felt the grit in her teeth. She unwrapped her head from the scarf and picked up her suitcase, knocking her flying bag off the bed and spilling out its contents.

Getting down on her knees she dragged the bag towards her and saw a pale blue envelope face down. Confused, she picked it up and was surprised to see her name written across the front in neat cursive handwriting.

She flipped it over and slid her thumb beneath the flap. Inside was a single piece of paper, folded over once. She opened it and her eyes drifted to the bottom to see who the sender was and her heart skipped.

Eos,

Remember that you are the mother of the winds, may they keep you safe and carry you back home.

Lovingly,

Your Tobias

Rosamund's skin rose with goosebumps and her heartrate skidded off kilter. *Your.* Her fingers lightly traced the word. He was waiting for her and he believed in her, and that was all the reassurance she needed.

The next morning the women gathered in the classroom to meet their instructors and begin their flight education. Rosamund expected a practical lesson but was surprised to find an arithmetic test being slid in front of her.

'This is just a little test to check you have the skills you'll need to fly a plane,' their instructor Bob "Mac" McKay said as if he was speaking to children and not women who had flown planes before.

'But we can fly planes,' one woman spoke up but Mac ignored her and kept walking around handing out tests.

Pearl and a woman called Ethel shared a look. Murmurs began snaking through the room as women consulted each other. Mac stopped short of sitting down and looked around the room.

'Is there a problem, ladies?' The whispers stopped and silence fell around the room. 'I didn't think so.'

'The men don't get these,' Ethel snarled quietly as Mac sat down and opened a form guide. 'My brother told me what he had to do before he became a pilot and it had nothing to do with an arithmetic test.'

'You have 30 minutes. No talking, no looking at the person next to you.' Mac pointed at the clock. 'Your time starts now.'

Rosamund didn't get a chance to answer Ethel as all the women put their heads down and started working on the test. When the time was up, every woman handed in completed tests to Mac. Rosamund was one of the last to hand hers in and he held her fingers under the paper, holding her in place.

'So it is true, we do have a real life movie star among us.'

His eyes roved over Rosamund's body, lingering on her chest. Rosamund bit her tongue but her cheeks heated in anger.

'I look forward to getting to know you better,' he said, holding her gaze for a beat and then letting her hand go.

Cheeks still hot, Rosamund spun on her heel and walked out of the classroom, her skin crawling, trying to avoid her instinct to kick the little man in the shins. She looked over her shoulder as she walked out of the classroom and saw Mac was still watching her, his tongue running over his lips.

THE WOMEN WAITED OUTSIDE under the shade of a large oak tree as the instructors went over their tests. As it turned out, the women weren't allowed to continue in the program if they failed the test. Mac whistled to them like you would dogs and called them back in. He waited till they were all seated and then stood at the front of the classroom.

'Congratulations ladies, you are one step closer to becoming pilots.'

Rosamund leant towards Pearl.

'Is it just me or does he seem disappointed we all passed?'

Pearl rolled her eyes and huffed. Mac then went through what they would be doing over the next few weeks. They would learn Morse code, memorize flight procedures, learn how to navigate without radar and meteorology. They also would need to learn how to fix an engine by pulling it apart and putting it back together. Mac smirked.

'Sorry ladies, but you're going to have to get your hands dirty.' He laughed, his eyes falling on Rosamund.

Ethel leant close to Rosamund.

'I'd watch out for that one, he seems to be keeping a rather close eye on you.'

Rosamund cleared her throat uncomfortably and started taking notes. She didn't have eyes in the back of her head, but every cell in her being agreed with Ethel: Bob McKay was not a man Rosamund wanted to anger.

THE FIRST FEW weeks for class 43-1 went quickly. The women were itching to get in the planes and actually fly, but their male instructors didn't seem as eager. By the end of the first month they fell into a routine. Not being part of the military, they had to supply their own uniforms once they realized their civilian clothes weren't working. Rosamund and some of the other women bought men's trousers and tightened them with a belt but it still wasn't practical. The pants swam on most of the women and they were harder to work in than their civilian clothes.

The women simmered with anger at the clear disdain shown by their male instructors. Some were great teachers and treated them as equals, others thought their time would be better spent teaching cats. Rosamund had largely managed to avoid Mac, but she still felt his eyes on her. Most of the men behaved themselves, but some of the girls, not so accustomed to the ways of men, found themselves the target of inappropriate behaviour.

The women became a tight unit, banding together to help each other. Rosamund had earnt the nickname Hollywood, thanks largely to Pearl, but she also had taken on a mother hen persona for the greener girls. Rosamund had seen a lot in her time at Warner Brothers and felt very protective of those who were more innocent.

The last task the women were being taught was taking the engines apart. Rosamund walked into the classroom, rifling in her bag looking for a book.

'Well, well,' Jane, one of the college graduates, whistled. 'It's about time we got a good looking instructor.'

'He's a fox.'

'He can take a look at what's under my hood anytime,' Pearl purred and Rosamund, looking at the instructor, felt her cheeks flash with heat.

'Well if it isn't the Titan herself.'

Every head in the classroom turned to look at her.

'If you wouldn't mind, Miss Winter, the audience is waiting for me, this time.'

'Oh ah,' she said as the group chuckled, all eyes following her as she scurried to a seat up the back. 'My apologies, Mr....?' she pretended to ask vaguely, as she sat, her cheeks still burning.

'Matthews. Tobias Matthews.'

*R*osamund listened to Tobias speak but none of his words made sense. Her mind swirled and swung between surprise, joy, his lips and worry. She was thankful that he'd twigged quickly that their association shouldn't become common knowledge and went on to treat her like every other woman there. Class adjourned for a break and Rosamund rushed out of the room, worried that a lifetime of acting wasn't going to cover what her heart was screaming.

Pearl found her under a tree halfway through a cigarette.

'Is there a man on green earth that doesn't want to ravage you?' she joked and pulled out a cigarette herself. 'You know no-one will try with him now because they don't think they've got a chance against you.'

'I don't know what you're talking about,' she said a little too quickly.

'Ah hunh,' Pearl answered. 'Blind eye Freddy could see the sparks flying between you two. Keep it under wraps though, we don't need to give Mac another excuse to fail someone.'

The women smoked in silence until they were called back to class.

Tobias had set up different engines on the tables and called the women to stand around. Rosamund tried to keep her distance from him as she was worried what she would do if she got close enough to smell his scent. He was wearing his coveralls over a shirt and she knew his shirt would be unbuttoned just one too many. She closed her eyes to try and control her breathing. They were scheduled to start taking the planes up tomorrow and she didn't want to give Mac or any of the other instructors a chance to keep her grounded. She would just stay away from Tobias. Easy.

The women broke up into groups to start taking the engines apart and Rosamund chose the table furthest away from Tobias. She could sense him before she saw him. He stepped up behind her and leant over her to look at what she was doing. She continued to tighten the bolt and tried to not breathe through her nose. She pursed her lips in concentration.

'You've done this before, Miss Winter,' he said and Rosamund could only nod.

'Clever man getting you on the tools as well as the cockpit.'

'Yes,' she said, wiping the sweat away from her forehead with the back of her hand. 'I had a good teacher.'

'He sounds like a very smart and good-looking man.'

The girls around her laughed and Rosamund played along. His smell of wood and leather hit her hard. He leant over and placed his hand over hers on the engine.

'You just need to crank this harder to make it tight and secure. Like this.' He levered his hand over hers and together they tightened the bolt. 'If it's not on correctly it could come off and then you're in real trouble.'

When he moved his hand off hers, Rosamund forced her eyes to remain downcast, the heat of his skin on hers remained. 'There you go, perfect.'

'Thank you, Tobias. Would anyone else like a turn?'

She handed the wrench over and wiped her hands on the cloth in her back pocket and stepped back from the table. Tobias walked around giving tips on the best way to drain the oil and fastest and most efficient way to fix certain issues that might crop up. By the time they had finished the sun was sitting low in the sky.

She was eager to leave to get an early night. A couple of B-17s were coming in the next day and the women were finally getting the chance to fly.

She could see through the classroom doors that Pearl was waiting for her under the tree, smoking, the dogs running around the field stretching their legs. She was about to step out the door when a voice from the shadows stopped her.

'I was hoping I'd run into you,' Tobias said, smiling.

'What are you doing here?' Rosamund asked.

'Jackie called in one more favour. Wanted someone she trusted to teach all of you about engineering. Been having a bit of trouble with some of the other instructors?'

Mac's face flashed into Rosamund's mind and she nodded her head.

'You could say that.'

Every fibre in her body wanted to run to him, to press her lips to his once more, to hear him call her Eos in person and not just in her dreams, but something stopped her.

'Good to see you, but I've got to go, my ride is waiting,' she said coolly. She began walking away but his words stopped her in her tracks.

'So we pretend that we don't know each other, is that it?'

Rosamund stopped but didn't turn towards him. They were the only ones in the classroom, the only light now coming from the setting Texan sun through the door, casting the room in a vibrant orange.

'Is this because I said no to having dinner with you?'

Rosamund turned to him, the pain piercing her heart.

'No, it's not about the dinner,' she said, annoyed. 'Although it has been a long time since someone said no,' a smile slowly spreading. 'I can't be seen to know or have any known connection with an instructor, it's not allowed.'

She watched as the bus arrived to take most of the women into town. Pearl had disappeared from view, the dogs now sitting in the back seat waiting for her.

'Rosie...' he said and pulled her into the shadows, holding her against him. 'Did you not get my letter?' He tucked her hair behind her ear and wiped at something on her cheek gently with his thumb. 'I always thought you were at your most beautiful like this. Wild hair and grease stained.'

He leant towards her but she pushed him back against the wall.

'I'm sorry,' she stuttered, moving backwards and making space between them. 'But we can't. I can't. It's hard enough with everyone asking me about Erroll bloody Flynn and Gene Kelly and Fred Astaire and is Vivien Leigh as beautiful as she appears on screen. I worked hard to be taken seriously here and I won't have whatever you think is between us, take this away from me. Now if you'll excuse me, I need to go home and prepare for tomorrow.'

She went to walk away but Tobias stepped forward, placing his hands on her arms gently.

'Look me in the eye and tell me.'

Rosamund took a deep breath and gave the performance of her life.

'There is nothing between us, there never was.'

She held his gaze for a beat and stepped out of his hold, her heart stinging at her lies. Tobias dropped his hands and stepped away from her, his hand dropping into a slow clap.

'And the Oscar goes to...' he looked as if he was going to

say something else, but he stopped, bent to pick up his bag and swung it onto his shoulder. 'Good luck tomorrow.'

He walked out of the classroom and Rosamund gulped for air, dropping to the floor, the tears falling hard and fast. She heard an engine fire up and speed out of the field, the stones from the driveway hitting the shed like shrapnel.

She only looked up when the sunset disappeared and a figure blocked the light. Pearl ran in and dropped to the floor.

'Are you ok? Did he hurt you?' she asked, looking Rosamund over, but she couldn't speak. It was if Pearl was speaking under water, the sound of her voice muffled over the sound of her thundering heart and the voice in the back of her head repeating *you stupid, stupid woman.*

CHAPTER 7

'*W*here, where did you come from?' Rosamund sniffled.

'I was hiding out back as I figured you might need a cover story as the only two people apart from me were both still inside. I hid around the back until I heard everyone else leave. What the hell happened?'

Rosamund thought about lying and say he had tried to grab a kiss but that wasn't fair to Tobias; he'd done nothing wrong except fall for her.

'Come on, tell me on the way home. Let's get you out of here before someone finds us.'

The women pulled the door behind them, the key still in the lock. Rosamund locked the door and took the key, putting it in her pocket.

'He'll never speak to me again,' she said as she climbed into the car. Martha leant forward and her rough tongue licked her ear, as if knowing that's what she needed. She leant her head back on the leather seat and Martha placed her head next to hers, puffing out air.

'So, you have met him before today!' Pearl hooted happily.

'Just my luck, the only man I've been attracted too since husband number three and he's already connected to you. Figures.' She started the engine and looked over at Rosamund. 'What's the story between you two?'

And Rosamund told her everything. Howard. Tobias teaching her how to fly and how to work on the engines. How he never once made a move on her until their kiss in the plane. And that this was the first time she'd seen him since.

'You, my dear, need a stiff drink. Let's get you home and bathed and into bed. I'm sure he'll forgive you and once the war is over you can go back to him and make lots of babies together.'

Rosamund closed her eyes, the night air cool on her hot cheeks and she wished that someone had invented a time machine so that she could go back and never had kissed Tobias Matthews.

After a light meal and a stiff drink with Pearl, Rosamund went back to her room to have a bath. As she threw her pants on the floor a tinny sound tinkled on the wooden floor and she looked down, confused. She bent down to have a look and saw the key from the classroom on the floor.

'Damn it,' she said and picked it up, the last bit of energy leaving her body. She'd have to take it back to him or he might get in trouble. She didn't want to be the one to have to explain to Mac why she had the key and not one of the instructors.

She flung open her suitcase and threw on a moss green tea dress with small gold and white flowers and grabbed her leather jacket to put over the top. She pulled on a hat that fell low over her eyes and quietly closed her door behind her.

She'd just sneak the key under his door, he was a smart man, he'd figure it out. But which one was his room? Her mind raced as she ticked off who was in the motel. Most of the Last Saloon Motel was taken up by the WASPs and only a few rooms were vacant. She stuck her head out the door and looked around the rooms. Most of the windows were dark, the occupants already asleep.

It was hopeless, she'd never know which one he was in. As she went to turn away, the key pressed into her palm, she saw him. He walked past her, not seeing her in the shadows, his feet crunching on the stones. He held a bottle in a brown bag in his hand and drank from it as he walked. She watched him walk towards the corner room on the other side of the motel and she tiptoed past the rooms on her side to get there. Looking to see if no one else was around she doubled back around the back of the motel and stood outside the window at the back of his room. She took a deep breath and held it, waiting to hear if he was walking towards the window.

'You know most people enter via the door,' a voice behind her spoke and she spun around startled. He gave her a lopsided smile and took a sip from the bottle.

'What do you want, Rosamund?' The use of her full name was like a slap to the face and she straightened her shoulders.

'Here,' she said holding the key up. 'You forgot this. I didn't want you to get in trouble for forgetting to lock the classroom. It's okay, I locked up for you.'

'Well, thank you for thinking of me,' he said sarcastically. 'It's nice to know you can think of someone other than yourself.'

Rosamund bristled and waggled the key at him. 'Here, take it.'

'Bring it to me,' he said, his tone daring her.

'You're a big boy, you can get it.' She went to throw it but he was on her before she got the chance, his hand over hers, the bottle he'd been drinking from discarded on the grass. His body slammed into hers and they fell against the wall, their hands still entwined.

'It's a tale as old as time,' he said his face inches from hers.

'What is?' she panted, her hands still above her head, her breathing ragged.

'The fool falling for the beautiful woman who will only break his heart.'

He threaded his fingers through hers, the key dropping to the ground and she squeezed his hands, his lips hot on her cheeks.

'You're not a fool,' she whispered.

He stared at her 'But you're not mine.'

'But I am,' she replied. 'I'm your Eos.' He dropped her hands and wrapped his arms around her body, pulling her into him, his lips smashing onto hers. She put her hands on the back of his head and ran her hands though his hair, pushing him closer to her. An unintelligible shout came from one of the rooms and they stopped kissing, both still breathing hard.

'Wait right here,' he said and ran away, leaving her leaning against the wall, a quivering mess. A few moments later he slid open his window and offered her his hand.

'Allow me the pleasure of a dawn?'

She climbed through the window before he'd finished talking.

SHE AWOKE EARLY the next morning, leaving Tobias a note reminding him to look for the classroom key somewhere outside and snuck away before dawn. The air was chilly and the morning sky bright. Not a cloud in the sky. That was good news for flying. She went back to her room, washed her face and got dressed in her coveralls.

She knocked on Pearl's door with breakfast and was greeted by her bleary-eyed friend. Pearl assessed Rosamund with a grin slowly spreading across her face and she stepped back, inviting her into her room.

'So I'm guessing you and teacher made up then.'

'Something like that. Now, get your ass in gear. We have planes to fly!'

Although Tobias was foremost in her mind, getting up and flying after months of being stuck in a classroom was the thing that put the extra spring in her step. When they got to the airfield the air was electric. All the women were buzzing. They lined up on the tarmac next to the B17. Rosamund walked underneath and around it, taking in its size and breadth. She had her hand and one foot on the ladder when Mac sidled up next to her.

'Eager to get on board are we? Shall we let you be the sacrificial lamb?' She turned her head towards him and swallowed the words she really wanted to say.

'I'd be honoured to be the first WASP in the air,' she said instead. His eyes narrowed and he nodded.

'Hollywood's up first. Take notes of what not to do, ladies.'

He walked behind Rosamund brushing his arm against her bottom and she pursed her lips in anger as he went to speak to other instructors. She began climbing the ladder, eyes narrowed in focus.

'You can do it. Rosie!'

'Show em' what a WASP is made of!'

The calls of inspiration continued even after she was in the cockpit and Rosamund's heart swelled. There was nowhere else she'd rather be right now. She pulled herself into the cockpit and looked around at the instrument panel.

She sat in front of the control stick and wrapped her hands around it. A thrill ran through her and she shivered.

'Bet that's not the first stick you've had your hands on,' Mac said close to her ear and she jumped with surprise, angry he'd startled her.

'Well, as I am a pilot, you'd be right' she answered, ignoring his true meaning. He sniggered and sat down in the chair next to her. 'Now, should I turn her on?' Mac smiled again and Rosamund rolled her eyes. 'Have you got any other innuendoes you'd liked to get out of your system because I'd like to serve my country and fly planes.'

He tilted his head watched her, his eyes narrowing in thought.

'You really do think you're going to help, don't you?'

It was Rosamund's turn to look at him bemused.

'Some of us will be making a difference.' They locked eyes, neither blinking in a silent standoff, daring the other to break their gaze first.

He sighed and pointed to the instrument panel. 'Show me if you've retained any of the information we've taught you.'

She closed her eyes and steadied her breathing as Tobias' calm voice floated into her head. She opened her eyes, a steely resolve flowing through her as she ran through her checks, flicking switches and reading dials. She turned on the first engine, then the next as she watched them all engage. As she took off and became air born she allowed herself a sideways glance at Mac but his face was unreadable. He made her land and take off over and over again and she was sure he was doing it to tire her out.

When she returned to the ground her arms were shaking, sweat pooling at the base of her spine, her chest tight from holding her breath. When she pulled the plane to a stop she could see the women on the side jumping and cheering. She looked at Mac but his face was unreadable.

But not even Mac could take this jubilant feeling away from her.

'Meet me in the classroom after lessons today and we'll go through a debrief. Send the next one up.'

Rosamund nodded and began her descent out of the plane.

The first face she saw as she turned around was Tobias who was grinning from ear to ear. 'Well done, Hollywood.'

She gave him a look but couldn't keep the smile off her face. 'That what you're calling me now?'

'Everyone else is, and I thought it was a fitting call sign. How'd it feel?'

By this time, she was surrounded by some of the other WASPs who wanted to know how it felt.

'It's heavy, really heavy, all the PT they've been making us do is for good reason! I had to use the blocks which as you can imagine went down well with Mac.'

Rosamund sat under a tree and watched as the next pilot went up, a pocket rocket called Peggy. Rosamund hoped Mac wasn't giving her a hard time and that she gave as good as she got.

The rest of the day was spent between the classroom, PT and flying. Once the first pilot went up the women were encouraged to study as much as they could because after a few flights they would be assessed. They took turns taking the planes up and Rosamund went up three times. By the time the daylight was fading her arms were weak and her head was light. The lack of sleep from the night before had finally caught up with her.

She walked into the darkened classroom and sat down on one of the tables at the front waiting for her verbal assessment of her flights from Mac. She stared at the clock, the voices from the other pilots fading as the last few people left. Pearl had left earlier to pick up her dogs but said she'd be back for Rosamund later. The door behind her closed and she swiveled to see Mac walking between the desks.

He sat down on the desk next to her, placing his hat beside him.

'I think we got off on the wrong foot,' he began keeping his eyes on the floor. 'I'd like for us to start over.' He looked up at her and gave a weak smile that fell short of meeting his eyes. 'I'd like for us to be friends if you think we can.'

Rosamund assessed him and his very sudden turnaround of emotions, her gut twitching that something wasn't adding up.

'I'd like very much for us to have a professional relationship,' she replied.

'It's an interesting word isn't it? "Professional". What's the definition of a professional?' Rosamund shifted on the desk to get a better look at Mac. She'd never seen him like this and she didn't know where this conversation was going.

'Well, I suppose the definition of a professional is someone who does their job no matter what the circumstances. They just get on with it.'

'Yes!' Mac said jumping up and standing in front of her. 'Doing the job no matter what is asked of them.' He raised his hand to Rosamund's cheek and cupped her face. 'I think you know a thing or two about that.' His hold on her face turned into a pinch as his thumb and forefinger squeezed her cheek. 'The Hollywood whore is what we call you. All actresses are whores.'

Rosamund jumped up, twisting her face out of his vice-like grip.

'Then I suppose you haven't met many actresses. I'm guessing my assessment is over then?' Rage coursed through her veins. She shook from rage and her inability to do anything. If she complained she would no doubt be kicked out of the program; after all, who was going to believe her?

He pushed her up against the desk and she leant backwards to try to put as much distance as possible between them. He ran his hand up her leg and cupped her buttocks with his hand.

'You tell me, is your assessment over?' He leant in to kiss her and Rosamund pushed him off and hurried towards the door. The last thing she heard as she burst through the door was Mac sniggering.

'See you tomorrow, Miss Winter.'

CHAPTER 8

'That son of a bitch!' Pearl said as Rosamund filled her in on what happened over dinner that night. 'Although it's no surprise. I've heard a few of the instructors making moves on some of the younger girls, but nothing as handsy. What are you going to do?'

'What can I do? If I complain I'll be kicked out of the program for sure and then I'll miss out on flying, not him.'

'Pfft, he's already missing out on flying, hence why he's trying to big man over us. Oh, he makes my blood boil,' Pearl said, swigging on her whiskey. 'Someone should make him pay.'

Rosamund shrugged. 'It could have been a lot worse.' She swirled the ice around in her glass, the whiskey now long gone, her thoughts turning dark as she thought about what he could have done to her while they were alone. 'I'm sure he only tried it on me because he thought I'd cave—being a whore and all.'

'Even the use of that word angers me, even if he didn't touch you. The assumption of it all. Even if you're not a saint,' she said winking. 'Well, I wonder what lover boy will have to say about it?' Pearl said her eyes crossing the room.

Rosamund spun around to see Tobias striding towards them. Her eyes went wide.

'You can't say a word, Pearl, to anyone, I'm trusting you.'

'But what if he hurts someone else?' Pearl hissed. 'And does worse than a hand on their ass?'

Rosamund looked back towards Tobias who had been stopped by one of the other instructors.

'Please don't tell him, he'll confront him and then we'll both be out of here.'

Pearl crossed her arms and huffed, her glass now empty as well. 'I think a good ass kicking would actually be good for him, but your secret is safe with me... unless he has a go at another girl.'

Rosamund said nothing as Tobias sidled up to their table.

'Ladies, how was your first day of flying the big girls?'

'Amazing,' they said in unison and followed with a laugh. Tobias sat down with them and shared a drink. They swapped flying stories and Tobias let them in on the gossip from the instructor's camp. It appeared Mac was not a favourite with them either.

'He hates me,' Tobias said as they ate some dinner together.

'Because you're so good looking?' Pearl purred.

Tobias laughed. 'You flatter me Pearl. No, because I live on the West Coast.'

'No, it's because you fly,' Rosamund said. 'He hates that you can leave soon and he'll be stuck here teaching us.'

The table fell into silence. When Pearl got up to got to the bathroom Tobias lightly touched her leg under the table.

'Can I see you tonight?' he asked quietly.

She felt a tingle low in her body and she longed to stroke the hand on her leg.

'I can barely lift my drink let alone do anything else,' she joked.

'Fair enough, you've had a big day. You did well, Rosie.' He lifted his glass and they clinked them together.

He waited till Pearl was back and excused himself. She watched him stop by a group of men who were all huddled over in a corner booth. When Pearl and Rosamund exited the restaurant Tobias came up behind them.

'I'll escort you ladies,' he said, looking over his shoulder. Both women took the arm that was offered to them.

'What's going on?' Rosamund asked as he hurried them down the street.

'They're reporters here to cover the lady pilots,' he said and turned his head towards her. 'But they've just discovered their lead story.' Rosamund looked over her shoulder to see flashes of light. 'Hollywood actress flies out of Hollywood.'

THE NEXT DAY by the time Rosamund and Pearl arrived at the airfield, the number of photographers and reporters had doubled. Jackie had called that morning. Rosamund was to look her best because she was now the poster girl for the WASPs and it was her job to convince everyone that they were an important part of the war effort.

When she stepped out of Pearl's car, she was Rosamund Winter, not Rosie. She smiled, flirted and charmed the press. She took them around and introduced them to the women, encouraging them to take as many photos as possible. She got up on the steps of the plane in her black pencil skirt and furs and turned around and smiled. She felt like an idiot, but Jackie told her to look the part.

Rosamund forgot about the article for a few days as they

continued to fly and go through assessments. She was practicing a march drill when Jackie called her over.

She walked over smiling but her face fell when she saw Jackie's expression. 'What's happened?' she asked, her stomach sinking.

'The article came out,' Jackie said, 'Roosevelt is happy. The Army Air Force not so much, but they never were going to be.' She gave a tight-lipped smile. 'You were my poster girl, and now you're not.'

Rosamund looked at her confused, wiping sweat off her brow with the back of her hand. 'But you just said that they liked the article.'

'You've failed flying,' Jackie said curtly, her arms now crossed. 'Apparently you are great on paper, not so good in reality.' She sighed, her face pinched. 'I'm sorry Rosamund but you need to leave the program.' Jackie gave her one last look and spun on her heel.

'Wait a goddamn minute,' Rosamund said grabbing her by the elbow. 'I've hardly been criticized, no feedback to the contrary telling me I was going badly. Who failed me?'

Jackie sighed again, pinching the bridge of her nose. 'Does it matter?' she asked. When Rosamund held her ground Jackie spoke again. 'It was Bob McKay who failed you. He said he'd tried his best, but you weren't up to it.'

Rosamund's nostrils flared as she snorted. 'Mac? I've been up with other instructors, what did they say?' Jackie gave her a funny look.

'You only need one instructor to fail you.'

'Ask another one, please. I will fly as many times as you want me to, but please ask another instructor for feedback.'

Mac's face after she rejected him flashed into her mind and she felt red hot rage.

'Please,' she pleaded. Jackie looked over at the planes taking off and landing and she smiled faintly.

'I'll ask around, but no promises. But if it turns out he has been… mistaken, I need a favour from you.'

Rosamund nodded her head. 'Anything.'

'I want you to fly into the Easter show in a few months' time as a propaganda stunt for the Army Air Force. Remind everyone that what we are doing is important. You can fly until then, but then I need you in California.' Rosamund nodded her head.

'Absolutely.'

Jackie gave her arm a squeeze and walked off. Rosamund held her breath and turned her eyes skyward. 'Please, please let me stay in the program.'

Rosamund got her wish to stay in the program. Word had gotten back to Jackie that some of the instructors were taking liberties with the women and when they rejected them, they were failed. Rosamund was angered to realise that some excellent pilots had probably been sent home incorrectly. After Rosamund, Jackie implemented the system where two instructors had to agree to fail someone before they were sent home.

Once she'd graduated with the first class of WASPs she was picking up planes straight from the factories and flying them across the country to air bases. Whenever she flew she had her small leather bag with her containing a few small toiletries as they never knew how long they'd be away. Rosamund once left thinking she'd be back that afternoon, only to return to Houston a week later. Each base she landed in gave her another plane to fly to another state.

The months passed quickly with Rosamund hardly seeing Tobias. They spoke on the phone and he'd meet her when she was in California, but the distance only strengthened their relationship. When Jackie reminded her of her Easter show obligations she was looking forward to a few days off and spending some uninterrupted time with Tobias.

'I'm looking forward to doing nothing for a few days,' she told him on the phone the night before she left for California.

The other end of the phone went silent.

'Tobias, are you still there?'

'I just can't believe that tomorrow you'll be in my arms again…and my bed,' came his answer.

Rosamund flushed and her skin tingled. She went hot and a wave of dizziness came over her, taking her breath away.

'Rosie? Rosie?'

Rosamund took a few deep breaths until her vison cleared. 'I'm here.'

'What happened?'

'Nothing, just a bit of a dizzy spell, nothing to worry about. I'm sure it's just because I'm so tired. A few days of rest will set me right.'

She looked at the calendar on the wall, the numbers not making sense. She traced her fingers over them trying to make them clear.

'Darling, I should go and get some sleep,' she said, her mind spinning. 'I'll meet you at the Easter show.'

'I love you.'

Her heart soared. 'I love you too.'

CHAPTER 10

San Francisco, California, USA
April, 1944

Tobias walked amongst the crowd, elated, the smile wide on his face. He'd woken up with it and it hadn't disappeared. He'd hardly slept the night before and he couldn't remember a time when he'd been this excited. He remembered the joy of waking up on Christmas morning as a kid, but this was much better. Rosamund was due to land at 10am. His Rosie. In a few short hours, she would be back in his arms. There had been talk that the war was ending. The tide had turned in the Pacific and the Allies were winning, and he hoped that meant they could start their new life together soon. His heart skipped off kilter at the thought of seeing her every day.

He walked over to the old football field where she would be landing and stood behind two women who were babbling about Rosamund's alleged relationships with various men in Hollywood. Tobias suppressed his smile behind his newspaper. If she was attached to even half the men they were talking about, then she was sleeping with half of Hollywood.

He'd kept the newspaper article about her arrival at the Easter show because it was a beautiful photo of her. Not that there were any bad pictures of her, but in this one she was pared back, wearing hardly any makeup, standing on the step of a plane, the wind in her hair, a joyous smile on her face. It was the Rosie he knew, not Rosamund Winter. The face he hoped to wake up to every morning of his life.

His hand moved to the small square box in his pocket and his heart swelled, the butterflies in his stomach rumbling. As the time neared 10am the crowd thickened with everyone wanting to see the movie star who had become a war hero. Tobias' heart gladdened to see a lot of young girls in the crowds. Rosamund was right, she was making a difference.

But 10am came and went and there was no sign of her plane. Tobias looked to the sky, the weather ideal for flying, and wondered what had delayed her. His mind raced with possible scenarios, all the time not allowing himself to think of the worst scenario. Faulty equipment? Something wrong with the plane to delay her leaving. The crowds grumbled and began to disperse, accusations that she couldn't actually fly and that it had all been a publicity stunt gone wrong. By midday Tobias found a quiet spot under a tree and sat. His chest tight with worry, he didn't want to miss her when she did arrive. The newspaper article was now twisted and shredded between his hands.

He waited until it was midnight, the sky as black as molasses. Easter came and went and Rosamund's plane never arrived.

After a week of waiting and searching with no sign of her plane, it was assumed that Rosamund Winter was dead. Tobias had called an Army Air Force buddy of his at the air base Rosamund had last been seen. He told him she had looked tired but was in excellent spirits and he'd checked her plane himself. Tobias trusted him. Rosamund had told him of other female pilots crashing after their planes had been fiddled with by their unhappy male counterparts, and he worried that may have happened to her.

After another week passed, Howard sent men to help Tobias find her. If Howard suspected his concern was more than that of a friend he didn't say anything. For two weeks they searched the flight path area and miles around but no sign of her could be found. A devastated Tobias returned home, his hopes and dreams crushed. The only woman he loved had disappeared without a trace, gone with the wind.

When he returned to his small apartment in Los Angeles he arrived to find a stack of mail piled by his letterbox. He collected the envelopes and threw them on his bench, some fanning out across the countertop, some falling on the floor. He grabbed a beer and slumped down on the floor and skolled the bottle. Once finished he threw the empty bottle across the room and it smashed against the wall. The ring box dug into his leg and he pulled it out, staring at it. He threw it and it landed on the fallen envelopes.

A yellow telegram envelope caught his eye amongst the bills on the floor. He bent and picked the paper up, his brow knitting with confusion. He ripped the edge off the envelope and pulled out the message.

His heart pounded. The writing blurred as his hands shook. The telegram was dated the day of the Easter show.

Darling,

I am safe and will see you soon. I will explain everything to you then. Until that day, please wait for me.

Love,

Your Eos

EPILOGUE

'Hello Tobias,' Rosamund said.

He froze, his knees sinking into the damp earth, his eyes unblinking, afraid that if he did, she would disappear. His mouth went dry and his throat tightened.

'Are...' he stuttered, 'are you real?'

She dropped the hand she was holding and fell to her knees to be on his level.

'Yes darling, I'm real.'

His vison blurred behind a wall of tears, her face breaking up into a kaleidoscope.

'I thought you were dead.'

'Mommy, why is the man sad?'

Tobias dried his eyes with the back of his hands and smiled at the little girl in confusion. He held out his hand for her to shake.

'Hello, my name is Tobias, but you can call me Toby.' The little girl hid behind the folds of Rosamund's dress, burying her face, but keeping one eye on Tobias. He looked at Rosamund sadly, his heart breaking.

'So, you're married,' he said.

Rosamund took the little girl's hand and patted it reassuringly.

'Tobias is a very good friend of mine. You don't have to be shy.' She looked back to him. 'Perhaps we should go inside and have some tea.'

'I think I need a whiskey,' he said, a little shaky and ashamed at how weak his voice sounded. She smiled and his heart shattered all over again.

'Yes, maybe whiskey would be best.'

They walked into the house, Rosamund and the little girl in front, Tobias behind. He directed them to the lounge room and he went into the kitchen and put the kettle on. As he fiddled with cups and saucers he stole glances at the woman in his house. She was more beautiful than ever, if not looking a little tired, but he supposed being a mother did that to a woman. The girl sat on her lap and she sang a little song to her. Tobias smiled when he realised she was singing the child a limerick for someone much older.

While the tea steeped, he poured two glasses of whiskey and handed a glass to her. Their fingers brushed and both pulled away sharply as if they'd both been electrified.

'How did you know where to find me?' he asked. He figured it was the easiest question to answer under the circumstances.

'Howard,' she said, not elaborating and Tobias nodded and took a sip of whiskey.

'Did he know you were alive?'

Rosamund turned to the little girl and smiled. 'Sweetheart, why don't you look out that big window over there and tell me how many different animals you can see.'

The girl, excited by her suggestion, popped off her knee

and ran over to the window. Rosamund looked back towards Tobias and smiled proudly. 'She's very smart for her age. She loves animals.'

Tobias looked at the girl with her dark hair and dark eyes, but she didn't look like Rosamund. She was pretty, but she didn't share her mother's features.

'Is she yours?' he asked and Rosamund looked at him, confused.

'Of course she's mine, I didn't steal her. She looks like her father,' she said as if answering his unspoken question. She turned her head to look at the child who pointed at chickens and horses and prattled in that language of small children.

'Where have you been?' he asked, unable to keep the agony out his voice. 'I thought you were dead. We all thought you were dead.'

His blood boiled at the thought she had deliberately stayed away from him. Despite the letter, she had made him think she was dead for three years. He jumped out of his chair, his hand stroking his moustache over and over.

'Why are you even here?' he asked. The little girl turned and looked to him, her big brown eyes wide and he smiled and she turned back to the window satisfied.

'Why?' he asked again quieter and Rosamund stood to join him, placing the empty whiskey glass down.

'Because I want Lou to meet her father.' Tobias stumbled back and she put her hand on his forearm, a dreamy smile on her face. 'Lou is your daughter, made and born out of love.' He looked down at her hand and saw a simple gold wedding band and he flinched.

'But how? That can't be.'

Rosamund smirked. 'I think you know how babies are made, Tobias.'

He pointed to her ring. 'My child. But she has another father.' He slipped her hand off his forearm and the spot where she had been touching him cooled. She looked down at the band and fiddled with the ring.

'A necessity so people didn't call her a bastard.'

Tobias scoffed and walked across to the large window at the opposite side of the room.

'How quickly you forget that I was an actress. His name was Thomas and he died in action and he was a complete figment of my imagination. Lou has never known her father.'

Tobias looked back towards the girl. 'Where does she think her dad is?'

'I tell her he is far away and that she'll meet him one day and he'll be so happy to see her.' Tears were pooling in her eyes and she gripped the armchair next to her. 'I wanted to contact you, to come to you a thousand times but I knew I couldn't.'

'Why couldn't you? You let me think you were dead!' he yelled and the little girl ran to Rosamund.

'Lou sweetheart, why don't you go and play on the porch out there with dolly. I'll be right here.'

She walked the girl out the door to the porch where she happily sat down in front of the window. Tobias looked at her face and suddenly realised who she looked like.

'She looks like my sister.'

'I always thought she looked like you. I was hoping she'd have your blue eyes, but…'

'She has your eyes,' he finished, his heart pinching. 'Why?' he asked again, still unable to stand near her.

Rosamund took a deep breath and he noticed how she clasped her hands tightly, her knuckles white.

'The last time we spoke I realised something. I was looking at a calendar and I realised I had missed a couple of my monthlies. I couldn't remember the last time I had one. In hindsight there had been other signs but I put it down to the long hours. After I dropped off the plane, I saw a doctor who confirmed I was pregnant and quite a few months along. That was a mixture of emotions.' She made an audible gulp. 'I called Howard and told him I was in trouble and he told me to fly to him. Everyone assumed an actress couldn't fly a plane so it wasn't such a stretch for people to believe I had crashed.'

A rage ran through him, his whole skin flushed with the sudden blood flow, his fists clenched at his side. 'Howard? Howard knew?'

Rosamund ran to him and hugged him but his arms remained by his sides.

'Darling, it was because of him that I could keep our baby.'

'So, you were embarrassed to be pregnant with my child. Did he know it was my child?'

He pushed her away gently and she shook her head, clasping her hands again.

'I never told, he did ask, he was furious that a man had done this to me and wasn't man enough to deal with it. You know Howard and his mood swings, I was worried what he would do if he found out it was yours, and I feared he would ruin your career forever and I couldn't let him do that.'

She sat back down in the chair, her hands pressed to her lips as if in prayer.

'Howard looked after us, ensured we remained hidden. There were many reasons I didn't return. I had intended to return earlier but I couldn't bring shame on the WASPS. If people found out I had a child out of wedlock, fell pregnant while as a WASP it would have reflected on them and they probably would have stopped the program.'

'They did stop the program. But not because of the women. Because the men started coming back.'

Rosamund nodded her head. 'So I heard.' She frowned

and jutted out her chin. 'Everything I did was for us and our daughter.'

Tobias couldn't help but release a reluctant smile. 'Defiant even when you're in the wrong.'

'I listened out for any scrap of news I could get from Howard about you. It was lucky he mentioned you'd bought this place just before you stopped working for him.' She looked out of the windows to look at Lou. 'When the war ended I was getting ready to leave, to come to you, but then Lou fell ill.' She turned her head away and silent tears ran down her face. 'I thought I was going to lose her... but she's tough, like her parents and she pulled through. I swear on her life I came to you as soon as I could.'

He looked out at Lou, his guard slowly melting. There was no denying she was his. The little girl could have been his sister and he shook his head at the marvel that was genetics.

'Will she like me?'

'She should, she's a mini you, she's nothing like me.'

She wiped her tears away with the tips of her fingers. He pulled out a handkerchief from his pocket and gave it to her.

She smiled her thanks and dabbed her eyes and looked up at him, a sly smile spreading on her lips. 'I told you I'd meet you at Easter.'

He felt the last of the frost around his heart melt and he chuckled through his own tears.

'You're three years late!'

She stood up and slowly walked towards him, her steps unsure. She stopped right in front of him, so close he could count her eyelashes.

'Can you ever forgive me? Understand why I did what I did? Be happy that we get this second chance?'

'What about Hollywood?'

'Hollywood is dead to me, I only want to be with you and Lou…if you'll have us.'

He looked at the woman who he had fallen in love with, who had broken his heart, let him believe she was gone forever and his heart thundered beneath his chest. It swelled as he imagined everything she had gone through alone, so she could protect everyone else around her. Protect his child.

'You once told me you wanted a simple life, away from the glitz and glamour of Hollywood. Is that still the case?'

She took his hands in hers and kissed them. 'That has always been the case. I'm your Eos. Let them believe that I'm dead darling, and we can start anew. A simple life, just you, me and Lou.'

He couldn't hold back anymore. He pulled her against him and eagerly crushed his mouth to hers, holding her close, afraid he would wake up and it would all have been a dream.

They kissed for time lost and what the future held, his hands in her hair, holding her the way he'd held her a million times in his dreams. Reluctantly they both pulled apart when Lou tapped on the glass giggling.

'Has she been in a plane before?' he asked hugging her tightly and Rosamund shook her head.

'I thought her daddy should be the one to do that first.'

He smiled, his heart skipping at the word daddy.

'Shall we take her into the dusk?' he asked, his eyes on his daughter.

Rosamund smiled. 'Let her meet her siblings the winds.'

THE END

~

Although this is a work of fiction, there are real people throughout the story. Howard Hughes, Jack Warner, Hedy Lemarr and Jackie Cochran are all real people and this work reflects the historical timeline where these people were and real events. There is the one exception of Howard Hughes talking about his idea for the Hercules. Due to the timeline of the story I have moved this conversation happening to 1943, but the United States Government actually approached him to build a transport plane in 1942. It wasn't completed until after the war but that, is a whole other story.

SARAH FIDDELAERS

~

Sarah is a writer, blogger and mother. She has a deep fascination with history and loves writing stories filled with the intrigue and romance of the past. Sarah was longlisted for the 2019 Richell prize and the 2020 Romance Writers of Australia Emerald award.

Sarah lives in the Macedon Ranges with her husband and five children. *Easter Promises* is her first published work.

Web: www.sarahfiddelaers.com

NANCY CUNNINGHAM

Nancy is a writer, research scientist and mother. Nancy has always loved stories about nature, science, history and love and has endeavoured to weave these into her stories. She writes across genres – including Historical, Romance, Crime and Science Fiction. Nancy has been a Romance Writer of Australia competition finalist (2019, 2020) as well as a finalist in the West Houston 'Emilys' (2020).

Nancy lives in Adelaide with her partner, daughter and several spiny leafed stick insects. She has published in Tulpa magazine and *Easter Promises* is her first published historical fiction work.

Web: www.nmcunningham.com

AVA JANUARY

~

Ava January is a writer living in sunny Brisbane with her sons and a Spoodle named Stroodle.

When she isn't breaking up fights over strangely shaped pieces of plastic, she can be found obsessing over Victorian era fashion (in the name of research, of course!) reading and writing stories with strong female leads.

Her first full-length novel, The Lady Detective - a light-hearted, romantic romp through Victorian England about a Lady Detective and London's most scandalous rake- will be released May 2020.

After embarking on a Bachelor of Creative Arts she fell heavily in love with writing and hasn't looked back. She was longlisted for the 2019 Richell prize.

Web: www.avajanuary.com

CLARE GRIFFIN

~

Clare begins conversations with "I love your shoes!" – often to complete strangers. Her work has appeared in MamaMia, Dolly, Kidspot, Poppy Renegade, Essential Kids, Somersault, Crossfire, SheGoes, Onya Magazine and many others. In 2016 she published her debut novel *Tumble* which became an Amazon best seller. The first chapter won the Freshly Squeezed C1 Blitz and became part of an anthology.

In 2017 her 10-minute play *The Karma Fairy* was runner up People's Choice Award as part of Gemco Players Take Ten Festival. Clare has also published several novellas and short stories such as *Happily, Ever After?* and *The Hunt for Scarlett O'Hara* a short story about the night Hollywood found its Scarlett.

Clare lives in the Eastern suburbs of Melbourne in a house full of men in the form of her husband, two sons and a retired greyhound.

Web: www.claregriffin.com